UP THE VICTORIAN STAIRCASE

UP THE VICTORIAN STAIRCASE

A London Mystery

Mabel Esther Allan

SEVERN HOUSE PUBLISHERS

This first world edition published in Great Britain 1987 by
SEVERN HOUSE PUBLISHERS LTD of
40–42 William IV Street, London WC2N 4DF

Copyright © 1987 by Mabel Esther Allan

British Library Cataloguing in Publication Data
Allan, Mabel Esther
Up the Victorian staircase.
I. Title
823'.914 [F]   PZ7
ISBN 0–7278–1489–3

8365103

SLS 11/87

Printed and bound in Great Britain
at the University Printing House, Oxford

Contents

1	Two Letters From London	1
2	We Arrive At Victoria Lodge	15
3	The Staircase	27
4	The Warwick Will	41
5	Interlude At Hampton Court	54
6	What Happened Near Henley	64
7	Accident Or Design?	80
8	More Danger	90
9	The Truth About George	101
10	Overheard In The Fog	114
11	Getting Away From Victoria Lodge	123
12	Alone By The River	132
13	Timandra's Nightmare	143
14	The End Of Danger	155

CHAPTER 1

Two Letters From London

That momentous day, a Saturday in the third week of September, began in quite an ordinary way. Except that the weather had turned hotter than it had been in July or August. By ten o'clock the temperature had soared into the upper nineties, and it was very humid.

I had promised to go up to Saks Fifth Avenue to change some gloves for Aunt Esther, but when she realised just how hot it was outdoors she tried to stop me.

'Please don't bother about the gloves, Timandra,' she said. 'It will do just as well Monday. I can go uptown myself then.'

But, unlike most New Yorkers, I never minded heat and humidity. I found something almost luxurious in great heat, especially when it would so soon be gone. Besides, I wanted to look for a certain new book. There were plenty of book stores on 8th Street nearby, but I had a favourite one near Saks, and it would be a chance to browse around.

So I went uptown into the ice-cold air-conditioning of Saks and the book store. I felt very contented as I came out of the second shop with the desired volume in my red nylon holdall. It was nice to earn money and be able to buy books: hardback books, newly published, not just paperbacks. For, now I was helping Uncle Serle in his office, he insisted on paying me. It was only supposed to be a temporary arrangement, although I insisted I *liked* working in a doctor's office.

My twin-brother Timothy was already settled at his art school, and that was the only thing he had ever wanted. I didn't want to go to any kind of college. I often felt guilty because I was so happy and so easily pleased. I felt that I ought to be protesting about something ... doing something really tough. I felt guilty because I was privileged, living in a loving, comfortable home. The only thing that really fascinated me was the world of antiques. In my spare time I haunted antiques markets and junk stores, went to special shows, read books on the subject. It started when I was fourteen, just before Father died. I bought a vase in an open-air flea market; it cost fifty cents. It was a little chipped, but for some reason it appealed to me. It was made of dark green glazed china, with a heavy base and yellow china roses climbing up the stem.

Tim, who had very definite opinions on colour and design even then, said it was hideous, but Father told me he thought it was Victorian and maybe one hundred years old. So I went to the library and found a book about Victorian furniture and china, and that led to learning about other periods. I had a vague dream of one day working among antiques. Even a real junk shop would be fun, for you never knew when something interesting or valuable would turn up among the ordinary or useless objects.

Meanwhile, I helped Uncle Serle, filing records, typing letters (with two fingers of each hand, but my English had always been good) and taking his receptionist's place occasionally. Wearing a white coat; greeting patients.

Dr Serle Dickson was not really our uncle. He and his

wife had simply been close family friends, but they were very dear to Timothy and me. They had given us a home when Father died and had treated us as if we were their own children.

As I crossed Fifth Avenue and walked up to the Channel Gardens of Rockefeller Center, I was thinking about this, and telling myself that the late autumn and winter were going to be good. Maybe, after Christmas, I'd take an evening course on antiques.

The high buildings, dimly blue, seemed to float in the heat haze, and when I looked along the Channel the RCA Building shot up, a pale, tapering finger, seventy storeys high. The RCA had been there all my life, and far higher buildings had soared into the sky, but I loved it best. It was so slender from that angle, so elegant.

Vivid orange and yellow marigolds filled all the beds in the Channel Gardens, and the place was crowded with tourists. I wandered along to look down on the Lower Plaza, hearing German and French spoken, and then clear English voices. Stabbingly, they reminded me of Father. I was a New Yorker born and bred, but he had been English.

A few minutes later I took the bus downtown, back to Greenwich Village. I was lucky enough to get the last seat, and, as the bus made its slow way through the endless traffic, I sat and dreamed about my father. He had been dead for nearly four years, but sometimes, as during that moment in the Channel Gardens, I could remember his voice: the voice that had remained a London one, in spite of many years in the United States.

My father, John Warwick, left London when still a young man, and he had settled in New York, eventually marrying a girl who had been born in Philadelphia. I only remembered my mother dimly, but I knew she had been pretty and a very warm and outgoing person. My earliest memory, and Timothy said his was the same, was of walking with her in Washington Square, under trees that were brilliant with the yellow-green of spring.

Father often spoke of London, though not of his family. He talked about the district of Holland Park, where he had lived, and of Buckingham Palace, Westminster Abbey, the River Thames. He had meant to take us to England one day, but he had died before this dream could be realised.

I only remembered him speaking of his home, Victoria Lodge, once, and that was on the day when I brought home the vase with yellow china roses. Then he said: 'I ought to know about Victoriana, if anyone does. Our London house was crammed with it. Some of the things were bought when the house was built in 1845, and successive generations added to them.'

When the bus reached 8th Street at last I stepped out on to the hot sidewalk. I had to buy a few things for my aunt before I went home. West 8th Street, the 'High Street' of Greenwich Village, was crowded with shoppers and tourists, and I didn't linger. I hurried into a delicatessen and made my purchases, then turned toward Washington Square, for I was fairly sure I would find my brother there.

The trees in the square had already turned gold here and there, and the towers of the World Trade Center downtown showed through the patterns of the leaves like vast, pale blue ghosts. The humid haze had thickened, though the sun still shone with a burnished, heavy glare. The square was very dusty, and noisy with playing children. It wasn't the way it used to be when we were children ourselves; there were far too many hippies and drug addicts. I was always a trifle scared of the vacant-eyed groups, and avoided them when I could. But Tim didn't mind. He said that he, like them, was part of the landscape, and they didn't take any notice of him.

I had been right. My brother was there, sitting on a seat under a tree, entirely absorbed in drawing a group of children. I guessed it was another picture for what he called his 'New York Kids Book'.

I sat down beside him with a murmured greeting, and the woman at the other end of the seat turned to stare at us both. I couldn't help noticing, though I was used to it. We are so very much alike, with the same bright brown hair, greenish eyes and straight noses. At the time Tim was wearing his hair quite long, longer than mine, and it was shining and clean, brushing the top of his cotton sweater.

'Phew!' I gasped, stretching out my feet in their dusty sandals. 'It *is* hot!'

'Thought you liked it?' Tim said. He had looked up, then continued with his drawing. 'Don't you think that child is just beautiful, Mandra? The one in the red dress. Look at her bone structure. Not Chinese, but some Eastern race. Maybe Malaysian.'

The child was certainly the most striking member of a varied group, and Tim's drawing had caught the curve of her cheek, the set of her eyes, with loving detail. I knew that my brother had great talent, and sometimes I felt sad that the artistic tendency had passed me by. Tim always knew what he wanted to do, even when he was quite young.

'I went to Saks,' I said. 'To change some gloves for Aunt Esther. And I heard English voices in the Channel Gardens. They reminded me of Father, Tim. I've been thinking of him all the way downtown.'

Timothy put a few more touches to the drawing, then

said: 'Let's go! I'm kind of hungry and it must be nearly lunchtime. Father . . . I often think of him, Mandra.'

We walked toward West 4th Street. The sidewalk was lined with pictures, for it was the time of the open-air art exhibition. I glanced at them as we passed.

'You ought to have exhibited something, Tim,' I said, but he shook his head.

'Maybe next spring. I don't feel I'm ready for it yet.'

We had lived in Greenwich Village all our lives, but, until a few months before, we had never had friends among the artists. Father's friends had mainly been connected with New York University. I think the Dicksons were the only exception.

Then Tim began to get to know young men and girls who lived in small, overcrowded studios, often in loft buildings. Some of them were utterly dedicated and never grumbled because they were poor, often with not enough to eat. They accepted me because of Tim, and I enjoyed their company, but I always felt an outsider. Maybe Tim did, too, because of the way he lived, but they knew he had talent and was in earnest.

Winter would find us going to parties; sitting on the floor, listening to music, arguing about Life. Things were never dull, and, as we approached the narrow old house where we lived, I was singing to myself. The front door was reached down three steps, and beside it was a brass plate that gave Dr Serle Dickson's office hours.

Quite unsuspecting that our lives were going to change utterly within the next few minutes, I led the way into the hallway, which seemed dark after the glare of the streets. Blinking, I looked around and saw two letters on the table. I picked them up, noticing the British stamps.

'Tim!' I cried. 'Look! Two letters for us from Britain. London postmarks. This one looks kind of important.'

Timothy peered over my shoulder.

'It sure does! Burrell, Gordon and Gray, Solicitors. Now why would London solicitors be writing to us?'

The living room door opened and Aunt Esther looked down at us from the top of a short flight of stairs.

'Hello!' she said. 'The mail came just after you left, Mandra. We're mighty curious about those two letters. How hot you both look! Why don't you come and have a cold drink before you think about anything else?'

I gave her the Saks bag and the food I had bought, then I stood in the middle of the living room, opening the important-looking letter. Timothy, less curious, or maybe more thirsty, busied himself mixing fruit drinks with large lumps of ice. He nearly dropped the glass he was just handing to me, for I gave a loud shriek of surprise. I read the first part of the letter rapidly again, astonished and . . . yes, my first feeling was one of utter dismay. Everything had been so safe and happy as we walked home through the humid, golden morning. But now . . .

'What is it?' Tim demanded. 'It's my letter, too, remember, Mandra.'

'We've been left a lot of money,' I said faintly. I found that I was shaking, and I desperately needed that drink. Holding the letter in my right hand, I reached out with the other for the glass. The ice-cold liquid poured down my throat deliciously before I spoke again. Tim and Aunt Esther stared in silence, then Tim said: 'Oh, come on, Mandra! Who would leave *us* money?'

'Well, we had an English grandfather, didn't we?' I asked. 'And he was rich – quite rich, anyway. We knew that.'

'We also knew,' my brother said calmly, 'that he never forgave Father for leaving London and settling over here.

Father always said we'd never see a cent of the money, and don't forget he was the younger son.'

'He did say that,' Aunt Esther agreed. 'But maybe things have changed.'

'I guess they have,' I said, frowning over the difficult legal phrases in the letter. 'Well, look for yourself, Tim. *You* read it, Aunt Esther. Translated a little, it seems to mean that our grandfather, Mr Brian Warwick, is dead, and that, apart from some small bequests and an annuity to his wife, he has left everything to us. And when his wife dies we inherit the London house, Victoria Lodge, and another house near Henley-on-Thames, in Oxfordshire. Mrs Maud Warwick *is* our grandmother, isn't she? While she's alive there's some special provision that all shall go on as before.'

Though I had offered them the letter, I continued to peruse it as if mesmerised. It was all so totally unexpected.

'I do wish he wouldn't use such legal terms,' I said fretfully. 'It makes the letter so hard to follow. But he ends more normally: "I suggest that you both fly over to London as soon as possible, when I can meet you and explain more fully. I understand that you are both eighteen, and I am wondering if you would like to consider making your home with your grandmother. Your grandfather's sudden death has been a great shock to her, and she is in poor health. Your uncle and aunt, Mr Basil Warwick and his wife, feel it would help her if she had the chance of getting to know you. In the somewhat unusual circumstances it would certainly be as well to come as soon as possible, whatever the length of your visit."'

Timothy whistled, and I noticed suddenly that Aunt Esther looked pale and troubled. But she made a sudden effort to smile and said: 'Well, it's surprising news, Mandra. But it's good news, in some ways. It's always nice to have money. Only . . .'

I handed the letter to her and took a few more gulps of my drink.

'It's such a coincidence,' I said shakily. 'I was thinking about Father this morning, and about London . . . the things he used to tell us. It was as if I knew something was going to happen. Yet I didn't know. I also thought what fun the winter was going to be. I was so happy as we walked from the square. I've always wanted to see the places he talked about, but this sounds kind of difficult. We won't really have to go *now*, will we, Aunt Esther? Maybe next summer we could all go together.'

'Sit down, Mandra. It's been a shock for you,' Aunt Esther said. She began to read the letter, holding it so that Tim could see it at the same time.

'It does seem to be true, but it's all mighty strange,' Tim remarked. 'Doesn't Uncle Basil get anything? We know very little about them, because Father never had letters from them, and he hardly ever mentioned his family. He didn't like them.'

'No, he didn't get on well with them,' Aunt Esther agreed. 'He once told me that they thought of no one but themselves, and all they cared about was material success. He seemed fond of his mother, but he said that his father and brother were both hard and narrow-minded. Your father was such a gentle, liberal man, and a dedicated scholar. I understand that his father, Brian Warwick, despised him because he wasn't very interested in making money, and he was very angry and upset when John refused to go into the family business when he left college. That was mainly why your father left London and came to the United States.'

'Then why should our grandfather leave all his money to us?' I asked faintly. 'A fortune!'

'I shouldn't think it's a fortune,' she said quickly. 'Not in today's terms. Mr Burrell says "a considerable sum of money, even when high capital transfer tax has been paid, and the sum equally divided." I'm very happy you're both to get the money, but it certainly is a shock, and will take a little time to get used to.'

'But we were so peaceful and settled,' I said, a little sadly. 'Oh, I guess it will be good to have money of our own, but right now I still want to help Uncle Serle. You don't really think we'll have to go at once, do you? You don't want to go until next summer, do you, Tim?'

My brother's good brow was creased in a frown.

'I don't know. It might be kind of fun. Seems we'll have to go soon and find out about it. In more detail, you know. Maybe sign papers – that kind of thing. It would be a pity to lose the money just because we don't want to leave New York.'

'I don't see how we could lose it,' I argued. 'We've inherited it now.'

The door opened and Uncle Serle appeared. He was a middle-aged man, with a kindly face, and he looked tired. He stared at us, then at the letter in Aunt Esther's hand, and demanded: 'What's going on?'

We started to tell him, all speaking at once, but he silenced Tim and me with a gesture and turned to Aunt Esther. She explained rapidly and gave him the letter to read. When he had read it, and reread a few phrases, he sat down heavily.

'Well, it's kind of nice that you've got the Warwick money, though we were going on OK without it. Your father left just about enough for your ordinary needs, and even if he'd left you without a dollar we'd have been happy to do all we could.'

My eyes filled with tears, for I loved him very much, and he had been so good to us.

'Couldn't we wait and all go together next summer?' I begged. 'I'd love to see London, but not . . . not so quickly, without time to plan.'

'There's my course at art school,' Timothy said. He was standing by the table, very straight and thin in his light coloured trousers and thin cotton sweater. I had always been sturdy, but he had been delicate as a child. He was tough enough at eighteen, but his whole vitality seemed to go toward his art. He hadn't my energy for general living. I knew suddenly that I could work on Tim, so that he wouldn't want to go to London. But did I really want to?

'You could study art in London for a time,' Uncle Serle said. 'Though of course we don't want to lose you.'

'Of course we don't,' Aunt Esther agreed. Her eyes looked suspiciously moist.

'I think you will have to go quite soon,' Uncle Serle went on. 'If only for a short time. Why don't we discuss it later? We don't have to decide right now.'

'There's the other letter,' I said, displaying the forgotten second envelope. I ripped it open and began to read. 'Gosh! It's from our aunt, Ann Warwick. That's how she signs herself. I'll read it aloud. "Dear Timothy and Timandra, About the time you receive this letter, you will also be hearing from our family solicitors regarding your grandfather's sudden death and the disposition of his money. He has left most of it to you. This was a great surprise to us, but we are delighted that, during his last months, he saw fit to try to patch up the old quarrel. He could do nothing for your father, but he has tried to make up for it by drawing you into the family. And we hope that this wish of his will soon be achieved.

'"We would be glad to see you both at Victoria Lodge as soon as possible. We feel it would cheer your grandmother to get to know you. There is plenty of room in this big house. It is really far too large for the present day. Your uncle and I and your cousin George, who is twenty, live in what is a separate wing, or annexe, built when the house was restored after the war. We would do our best to make you welcome. Just let us know the date and time, and your Uncle Basil will meet you at the airport."'

I stopped abruptly and a short silence fell. Then Tim said: 'I don't get it yet. It seems as if her husband and son have been passed over in the will.'

'Maybe they've enough money not to mind,' Uncle Serle remarked. At the same moment Aunt Esther asked if we didn't want to eat lunch, and I realised that I was very hungry.

'But I don't understand how they knew we existed,' I said. 'If Father never wrote them . . .'

'When your father died,' Uncle Serle said slowly, 'and you came to live with us, I thought it right to explain the circumstances to your grandfather. I had no reply to my letter, and I stopped worrying. We were very happy to keep you.'

'And we were happy to be here with you,' I assured him warmly. I felt a mixture of sorrow, doubt and excitement. 'Oh, life was so safe and ordinary, and now we don't know what will happen. I don't think I want the money. Can't we write and say someone else can have it?'

Tim made a sound of protest, and Uncle Serle said: 'That would be silly. Whatever we decide for the immediate future, you know that this will be your home for as long as you want it.'

'Oh, don't!' I gasped. 'I shall cry again.'

'That would be silly, too,' he said, smiling at me. 'I can easily get temporary help in the office, and think what fun you could have in London, Mandra. All those antique shops! And if you both decide that you want to stay there . . .'

'We don't know these people,' I protested. 'And if Father didn't like them, why should we?'

'Give them a chance, anyway.'

'I haven't any real talents,' I said. 'But I want to be useful. I wouldn't like to turn into an idle rich person. You'll have to keep it from your artist friends, Tim.'

Tim grimaced; he saw the point of that all right. Our present circumstances had been bad enough, when placed against the privations of many of our friends.

'I guess we won't tell them yet. If we go to London, we'll say it's just for a visit to meet relations. I thought your future was all mapped out, Mandra. You're going to marry before you're twenty.' He grinned at me rather unkindly.

'I was fourteen when I said that,' I pointed out. 'I can marry *and* be useful: do any kind of job . . . learn things. I believe in Women's Liberation. I'll always have a life of my own.'

'You'd just had your first date. Remember?'

'Yes, I do remember. He had spots and was terribly shy. I certainly haven't met the right man yet,' I said, with dignity. I went slowly upstairs to tidy my hair and wash my hands before lunch.

We lived in the whole of the tall, thin house. My charming room had a view of West 4th Street. I went to the window and leaned on the sill, staring at the church opposite. Then I turned and wandered slowly around. My 'collection' was on white shelves – the yellow rose vase, a Victorian pincushion, a fan, three little china dancers, a chipped mug that commemorated Queen Victoria's Jubilee: about thirty cherished objects, excitingly discovered and bought for very small sums of money.

There were my books, too: a *Dictionary of Antiques, Regency Furniture, Queen Anne Furniture, Victorian Houses and Their Contents, Collecting Victoriana* – two rows of titles, and I could add to them the book I had bought that day, *The Great Houses of England*.

Oh, only a short while before I had been so untroubled, and now, it seemed, Tim and I had money. Maybe, in the future, I could buy *real* antiques, not search everywhere for small personal objects costing only a dollar or two. But I felt a wave of sorrow because of that lost joy.

With the money we had also inherited problems. The thought of the family in London alarmed me. If we could wait until next summer, and all go together, that would be fine. Excitement stirred in me at the thought of seeing London at last, but I didn't want to be hurried.

The future was not the one I had expected an hour earlier. It was all very strange and rather upsetting. Uncle Serle would advise us, and it was comforting to know that we would always have a home on West 4th Street.

CHAPTER 2

We Arrive At Victoria Lodge

For two hot and windless September days the matter hung in the balance. Should Tim and I go to London almost at once, or should we wait until next summer, when the Dicksons might be able to accompany us?

My moods hovered between excitement and unhappiness. I was really scared by the thought of facing our father's relations without any support, but London did beckon. It would be so wonderful to walk the historic streets, and to explore the famous buildings. I could go to Hampton Court . . . four hundred years old, or more. And there was all the rest of England; those great houses described in the book I had just bought. Knole, Chatsworth House and many more, probably easily within reach of London. There would be antique furniture in the right settings, and porcelain and pictures. Though I had thought of England so much because of my father, and tried to learn all I could of its treasures, I don't believe, until then, the chance of my going had ever been more than a dream. And now it was a dream that could be realised almost at once, but at the price of living with strangers, and strangers who might not be friendly, in spite of Aunt Ann's efforts to sound welcoming.

Uncle Serle and Aunt Esther tried hard to hide their dismay at the thought of losing us, but I knew how much they minded. But, as Uncle Serle said, it was most unlikely that we would want to make a permanent home at Victoria Lodge. If we found that we liked the Warwicks we could maybe spend a couple of months with them each year, and it wouldn't hurt us to widen our horizons by getting to know another country. Especially as we half belonged there.

'But the Warwicks might try to keep us,' I said, voicing one of my fears.

'They really couldn't do that,' Uncle Serle said quickly. 'You're both eighteen; not children. You may not be able to handle the bulk of the money until you're twenty-one, but the Warwick family has no real claim on you, and certainly no power to keep you there against your will. Why don't you go for three months? That will give you time to find out how you feel.'

'But can you really find someone else to help you in the office?' I asked.

'I guess so. I'll employ someone temporarily, and then, after Christmas, if you really want the job . . .'

'Yes, I do,' I said. 'You know, I've been thinking maybe I can use most of my share of the money to do some good. I don't know how yet, but there might be a way.'

'Well, don't be too hasty about it. In fact, I'm sure you won't be allowed to make decisions of that kind for some time yet,' Uncle Serle said gravely.

Timothy prowled restlessly around the room.

'I'd really like to take a look at London,' he said. 'Maybe we could take a trip over to Paris as well. I've always wanted to visit France. And, if there's money now, I can go to really good teachers; the very best in London or Paris. I could even go to Italy.'

'So you really want to go, Tim?' I asked. 'Right now, I mean. I know you've always wanted to travel.'

'Yes, I guess so,' he said. 'I'm not keen on meeting the Warwicks, but I want to see the art museums. Victoria Lodge is right in London; in North Kensington. There's the Tate, and the National Gallery, and the Wallace Collection. And all kinds of special exhibitions. I could see them all quite easily once we've done the business with the lawyers. The family needn't bother us.'

'I don't see we could shake them off that easily,' I said doubtfully. 'We must always remember that Father didn't like them. Well, his mother was OK, I suppose, but think of the others. They may hate us. It would be natural, as we've got all the money.'

'That will does sound kind of mysterious,' said Aunt Esther. 'Serle, I wish you could take a short vacation and fly over to London. You could find out more, and say the twins will go later. That might satisfy the lawyers.'

'I can't, my dear,' he said. 'I'm much too busy. It's a difficult decision to make, but I feel they should go. Tim wants to go, and Mandra will enjoy it when she gets there.'

So airmail letters were sent to Burrell, Gordon and Gray, and to the Warwicks, saying that we were flying to London on 3rd October. The Warwicks were told that we would arrive at Heathrow airport at six o'clock in the evening.

Once we had made the great decision, Tim returned calmly to his work at the art school. I, much less calm – in fact, restless with excitement and a vague, nameless dread – was out a good deal, for Uncle Serle found a temporary secretary very quickly. I walked the streets of Manhattan with eyes that nostalgically noted every detail, for soon my native city would be more than three thousand miles away. That other city . . . would I learn to love it, and to feel I knew it well?

Oh, yes, increasingly I was thrilled to think of all the new things we were going to see, but I still minded leaving my home and friends, especially my current boy friend, Bill, who was a student at Cornell. I was not in love with him – if I had been it would have been even harder to go – but he was good-looking, and intelligent, and I liked him. I thought maybe it might even turn into love; who was to say? Sometimes, during those last days in Manhattan, I wondered if it already had. Certainly Bill was very sorry to think of losing me, but he seemed sure we would be back even before the three months were up. Bill was in the secret about the money, for he had no connection at all with the artist crowd. He thought it was nice about the Warwick inheritance, but he was not envious, because he came from a family with plenty of money. His father was a very successful businessman.

New clothes were needed for London, because most of our things were very shabby. I looked in dismay at my old winter coat and sweaters. I pictured London as almost always cold and wet, with a great deal of fog. Aunt Esther took me shopping and bought me two new dresses, sweaters, trousers and a very soft and luxurious fur fabric coat.

'The coat is a goodbye present,' said my adopted aunt, trying not to sound sad. She bought Timothy a heavy overcoat and warm sweaters, for she, too, believed that the London climate was even worse than the New York one in winter. Not so many degrees of cold, maybe, but so damp.

I felt rather remote from Tim during those last days at home. I resented the fact that he was taking it all so lightly and quite refusing to worry about the Warwicks. The only thing that seemed to trouble him at all was that he now had money, while his artist friends were mainly so poor. I was certainly far from my normally placid and contented self. I was even secretly scared of the flight, for it would be my first. I told myself that people were flying all over the world every minute of every day, but it didn't help much. Tim, who had made two flights with school parties, didn't even mention it.

Uncle Serle had bought round-trip tickets for us and I tucked mine away safely. I was relieved to know that we could return any time if we weren't happy with the Warwicks.

Our packing was done and the moment finally came – very early in the morning – when we left home and drove out to Kennedy airport. On 3rd October the weather was still warm, golden and windless, with just a few leaves dropping off the trees in Washington Square. It seemed incredible that we were going so far away, and everything settled into a state of unreality.

There were no problems at Kennedy. Our luggage disappeared at once, and Uncle Serle led us to the duty-free stores, saying that it might be a nice gesture to take perfume for our grandmother and Aunt Ann, and whisky for Uncle Basil.

'What about George?' I asked, dazed, but still remembering that we had an unknown cousin. And Uncle Serle laughed and said maybe he'd like Scotch, too.

We all parted at the gate, just as passengers were called to board the plane. I had vaguely imagined us walking out across the tarmac to reach the plane, the way you see people going on television and in movies, but it wasn't like that. We walked along several passages, then through a door and we were on board, without ever having gone outdoors. A charming hostess greeted us and said that as the plane wasn't fully booked we could each have a window seat if we liked. So I settled one side of the aisle and Tim the other, right in front of the tourist class section.

I wasn't sure I wanted a window seat; maybe it would be better not to see all that sky below. The strain of the past few days, the excitement, and still that vague dread of the Warwicks, suddenly made me feel exhausted. I glanced across at Timothy and saw that he looked quite calm. He was even groping in his holdall and bringing out some of the literature about London that the British Tourist Authority had provided.

The great engines began to throb and we taxied along the runway. I dreaded the moment of take-off, but when it came it was an astonishing thrill. The great thrust into the air left me gasping and excited, not scared any more. I was conscious of the plane's great power . . . a modern magic carpet to carry us across the ocean to the Old World.

When the order came to unfasten seat belts I reached for my own holdall, and balanced it on my knee while I searched for the London guide book I had bought. The plane gave only the very slightest of lurches, but the holdall slid sideways and fell, spilling its contents in front of the two empty seats beside me . . . guide book, London street map, an extra scarf and a good many other small things. I bent and began to retrieve the things within my reach. I didn't yet feel safe enough to stand up and get the small toilet bag that had shot right out into the aisle. The hostesses were busy starting to serve drinks, and Tim hadn't noticed. But someone else had. He rose from one of the seats behind Tim, handed me back my bag, then quickly scooped up the rest.

'I think that's all,' he said, smiling.

'Oh, thank you very much,' I said, smiling back. He was a very attractive-looking young man, fair and tall.

'Mind if I sit beside you for a while?' he asked. 'It's kind of dull sitting alone.'

'I'd like it,' I said. 'Tim's absorbed already. He's reading about art museums. He's planning to see them *all* while we're in London.'

He laughed. 'Is he your twin? I saw you at the airport. Was that your mother who was with you? I've seen her before. I believe she's on one of my mother's committees and they meet sometimes at our apartment. I'm Norris Carey, and we live on East 38th Street. Mother's involved in all kinds of things.'

I stared at him. It really was a small world, and it was strangely comforting to meet someone who knew my aunt, however slightly. 'Is her name Kathleen Carey? Oh, then I've heard Aunt Esther mention her. She's only an adopted aunt, but we live with the Dicksons. We haven't any parents. Yes, Tim is my twin. Our name is Warwick, and I'm Timandra.'

'*Timon of Athens*,' he said promptly.

'You're about only the third person who's ever known,' I told him. 'Father was very fond of Shakespeare. I'm glad he chose a pretty name. It might have been Calpurnia.'

'Or Portia or Nerissa, I suppose. They're quite nice. Timandra was a lady-in-waiting or a serving maid, wasn't she? I just remember her in the list of characters. I've never seen the play.'

This somehow gave him high marks. Norris went on to say that he was taking a vacation in England for one month.

'I've worked in my father's business since I left College,' he explained. 'He's a printer, principally of art books. It really is mainly a vacation, but I'm hoping to take a good look at British books, and maybe visit some English printing works.'

I told him that Timothy was studying art, and somehow, before very long, I had told him much more. About Father, and the Warwicks, and the strange will, and how I had mixed feelings about going to London. It was extraordinary how the fact of sitting beside a stranger in a plane thirty-five thousand feet above the Atlantic Ocean could so quickly result in a feeling of warm intimacy.

He was very sympathetic and interested, and he told me that he, also, liked antiques and had a collection of old paperweights. But, while we talked, I was conscious of that vast, incredible world of blue sky and great white clouds outside the seemingly frail windows of the plane.

After a time the Captain came along and began to talk to us, and, when he heard that it was my first flight, he asked if I would like to go on the flight deck. Awed, and a little scared again, I followed him to that very small space in the nose of the plane. He introduced me to the rest of the crew and explained the instruments, but the thing that impressed me most was that his seat was empty, and the plane was flying unaided through the incredible beauty of the clouds. The earth seemed very small and remote then, and I quite ceased to worry about the Warwicks.

When I returned to my seat Tim had moved over and was talking to Norris. We all sat together after that, and I began to wish that the flight could go on forever. But I had to think about the family again, because London was getting nearer every minute. In thirty minutes we would be there.

But then came the news that there was fog at London airport.

'Maybe we'll be delayed. Maybe we'll have to land somewhere else,' I suggested hopefully.

'I guess that would be a nuisance,' Norris remarked.

'But it would delay meeting the Warwicks. I really am kind of scared of them,' I confessed.

'You may even like them,' Norris said.

But it seemed that, after all, there was not going to be any delay. The fog was fairly bad in patches, we were told, but not dense. The signal came to fasten seat belts. I wished that I could hold Norris's firm-looking, suntanned hand. He seemed an anchor in an unstable world; our last link with America.

I was glad when he said: 'Why don't we meet again? I know London a little. We might go to places together.'

'Oh, yes. That would be nice.' I hoped I didn't sound too eager.

'I'll call you in a day or two then, if you'll give me your address. The number will be in the phone book.'

'It's Victoria Lodge, Plane Tree Walk, North Kensington.'

Norris Carey wrote it down, then gave us the name of a hotel near Sloane Square. And while we were exchanging these details the plane had landed quite safely. As we emerged into cold air and clinging fog, I breathed deeply and clutched Timothy's arm. We had lost Norris Carey in the scramble to leave the plane and only saw him in the distance as we waited for our luggage.

'Oh, Tim, can you really believe we're in London?' I cried. 'Maybe Uncle Basil hasn't been able to come because of the fog.'

But, when we followed our porter into an outer hallway, we immediately saw a short, grey-haired man signalling to us. I think, until then, I had kept a faint hope that he might look like Father, but he didn't. He came forward and shook hands. His voice was quick and rather harsh.

'You're Timothy and Timandra Warwick? How do you do? I'm your Uncle Basil. I'm glad to meet you both at last. How was the flight? This fog's a nuisance. Americans always expect fog, I know, but really we get very little nowadays. It's only patchy, though. We'll make it all right.'

He gave us no time to answer, but turned and led the way out of the building and into a multi-storey car park. The car turned out to be a Jaguar, almost new, and Tim seemed impressed. I wouldn't have cared if it had been a twenty year old Ford.

Uncle Basil put me into the front seat, and Timothy settled himself in the back with our hand luggage. When it was too late, I realised with dismay that I would probably have to do all the talking.

But Uncle Basil seemed disinclined for conversation. Perhaps he needed all his attention to drive the car out of the airport complex, which seemed like a whole city. Then we were out on a wide and busy road, and I felt my neck aching with tension. Most of the time my hands were clenched. It was alarming to be driven on what seemed the wrong side of the road.

Occasionally, in the dim, foggy light, I glanced at my uncle. He had rather thick features and a heavy brow; a mouth that looked hard and without humour. Not an appealing face at first sight, and probably it wouldn't be on later acquaintance. I told myself that it was far too early to make up my mind about him, but that he and Father could have been brothers . . . It seemed impossible.

After we had been driving for some time the fog thinned. It was growing dark, and lights began to shine out clearly.

'That's better!' Uncle Basil said. 'You must forgive

me. I hate driving through fog. Well, I must say it's very pleasant to meet poor John's children. Not children now, though, are you?'

'We're eighteen,' I answered stiffly, not liking 'poor John'.

'Our son, George, is looking forward to meeting you both.'

'Does George have a job?' Tim asked.

'He sells cars,' Uncle Basil explained, a trifle ruefully. 'Tries to sell 'em, one might say. He wouldn't come into my business, but I didn't try to force the boy. That way lies trouble, as we saw with your father.'

'Father was very happy at New York University,' I said. 'After all, he was a scholar – not cut out for business.'

'We were as different as chalk from cheese. Never had a thing in common. That sometimes happens in families.'

'You worked with your father? With Grandfather?'

'Yes, I did work in the family business for some years,' Uncle Basil admitted. 'Then –' he gave a harsh laugh – 'I cut away. Foolish of me, but I couldn't get on with the general manager, and I felt that one of us had to go. No chance of Murray going, since Father doted on him. So I started up on my own. I did very well, but the old man took it hard. Second family black sheep, you might say! Not that we quarrelled or anything like that. We went on living at Victoria Lodge. But you see what happened when the old man died? Cut me off with a shilling, as we used to say. Actually, it was fifty pence. Not that it matters, so don't give it a thought. I'm doing very well.'

It seemed likely that he was, with such an oppulent car, but I felt very uncomfortable, not quite understanding the speech. I looked out at what I could see of the London streets. Not very much, for the fog was wreathing thickly again.

'Kensington High Street,' Uncle Basil explained. 'Nearly there now. I expect you'll be glad.'

I nodded. Being in England seemed like a dream, or just possibly a nightmare. I was very tired and already homesick.

We turned left from the busy main road, and after a few minutes I could see big houses, with steps and pillared porticoes. There was suddenly no more traffic, and the houses looked remote and unreal in the fog.

We drove left again, into a street where there were trees and widely-spaced buildings, dimly seen, then took another turn into a short, narrow lane, unexpected in what must be the heart of the city. We passed through wide open gates and up a short, curving drive, bordered with high dark shrubs. The headlights, sweeping around, suddenly picked out a big house; I had a brief glimpse of heavy gables and what seemed to be a turret at one end. There were no lights in any of the windows, and when the car headlights were switched off the house itself was obliterated.

'Welcome to Victoria Lodge,' said Uncle Basil.

CHAPTER 3

The Staircase

Complete darkness lasted for only a few moments, then an outside light came on. The front door began to open, and Uncle Basil said: 'They heard us. I'll put the car away later. Come and meet the family.'

I longed to know what Tim thought, but there was no chance then of finding out. I scrambled stiffly from the car, saying to myself: I was right. We shouldn't have come.

We followed Uncle Basil up four wide stone steps. The front door was massive, thick wood embossed with iron, and then there was a second door, with panes of stained glass. The hall beyond was square and gloomily lighted. There were people, but for some moments my attention was not on them. I was dumb and breathless with astonishment, for the place did not seem to belong to the nineteen-eighties. Father had said that his home was filled with Victoriana, but that was years ago.

Furniture and objects in their natural setting . . . I saw them then: heavy wooden settles and chests, a Victorian sofa; tall, carved stands on which stood huge china pots holding plants with shiny leaves. And, in the background, a massive staircase, with great carved newel posts, went up into darkness.

Uncle Basil was speaking, and then, at last, I really noticed the people: a middle-aged woman in a smart beige dress, a young man and an elderly woman in black.

Just for a second I thought the elderly woman must be our grandmother, and was dismayed to find her so like a witch, with a sharp little face and straggling white hair, but it seemed that this was the housekeeper and family retainer, Nancy Cheam.

'So you're Timandra?' said the woman in the beige dress. 'I'm your Aunt Ann, and this is your cousin George. What a nasty night to arrive on! No wonder you look so cold and bewildered. Goodness, how alike you both are! It's quite uncanny. And this is Nancy Cheam. She knew your father, of course. She's been here since she was fourteen. Long before *my* time.' And she laughed rather affectedly.

George, who had been lounging near the foot of the staircase, came forward and offered his hand to each of us.

'How do you do, cousins? Or should I say "Pleased to meet you"? Welcome to London Town.'

'Oh, we're quite civilised. We say "How do you do?"' I assured him, and then I felt uncomfortable, because I wasn't usually rude. But I didn't like the look of him very much, and his handshake had been limp. He was, however, part of our new family, so I added hastily and untruthfully: 'It's very nice to be in London.'

The old witch, Nancy, had come forward slowly. She had bright, darting eyes that looked almost black, and she didn't seem overjoyed by our arrival.

'I suppose you want your dinner?' she enquired. 'We're late tonight on your account. 'Arry'll bring in the luggage, Mr Basil, don't you worry. They'd better go in and see the mistress. She's impatient to meet Mr John's twins.'

'Don't take any notice of her,' Uncle Basil whispered, as Nancy disappeared into the deep gloom at the back of the hall. 'She's a cross old thing and says just what she likes. But we're lucky to have her. She and her husband keep this great place running, helped by a young girl. We had a nasty moment when we heard that the old man had left them some money, but they've shown no sign yet of wanting to leave us. No one can get domestic help nowadays, as you probably know. And not many houses as big as this are lived in by only one family. They're usually turned into flats now.'

'Nancy adores the very ground we walk on,' George remarked lightly. 'She bullies us unmercifully, too. There aren't many left like Nancy, and she's getting very old. She's a bit . . . you know.' And he touched his head.

Both his father and mother frowned at him.

'She still has all her wits about her,' Aunt Ann said. 'Don't listen to George.' She moved toward a door on the right. 'Well, come and meet your grandmother. She isn't too good. She hasn't got over the old man's death yet, and sometimes she seems to be living in the past. Her rheumatism is bad, too, in this damp weather. Then, as soon as you've spoken to her, you'll want to go up to your rooms.'

I caught Tim's eye as we followed Aunt Ann. He winked reassuringly, but I could not smile back. I was very cold – clearly the house was not centrally heated – and my feeling of uneasiness was growing with every moment that passed.

The room into which we were led was huge and very high, and gloomier than the hall. There was a great deal more Victorian furniture, with a large television standing incongruously to one side. The only light came from a tall electric lamp near the fire, and, in a deep chair close to it, sat an old woman. At first she was half-hidden by a screen. I don't know what I had expected; maybe, by then, a Victorian bonnet. But I had a surprise. She was old, of course – well over seventy – but her white hair was elegantly arranged, and she was wearing a beautiful dark red robe made of rich velvet. She held out a slender white hand, and smiled up at us more warmly than anyone had done so far. Her eyes were like Father's.

'Well, I never!' she cried, in a low, attractive voice. 'Timothy and Timandra! John's children. My dears, this is a wonderful day for me. I always wanted to see you, write to you, but Brian was a hard man in many ways. He's dead, you know. Did you know that?' Her face suddenly looked older and more vague.

'Yes, Grandmother, we knew,' Tim said gently. 'He left us most of his money.'

'So he did. I'm glad of that. He must have forgiven John. How pretty you are, Timandra! But you're not like your father.'

'We look like Mother,' Tim explained.

'She must have been a good-looking woman. Of course we never heard . . . But how cold you both are, and you must be hungry. We can talk later. We'll have all the time in the world. Ann . . .'

'Yes, I'll take them upstairs,' Aunt Ann said quickly. 'I'm afraid Nancy is getting cross about dinner.'

When we returned to the hall an old man was struggling with our luggage. He was introduced as Harry Cheam, Nancy's husband. Tim took two of the suitcases and followed Aunt Ann up the great Victorian staircase. I took the holdalls and hesitated at the bottom of the flight. The treads, very wide, were covered with dark red carpet. Halfway up the stairs turned, the outer banisters carved all the way up in patterns of flowers and birds. The whole was far too heavy for real beauty, but it was certainly a wonderful period piece. The strange thing was that I didn't want to mount those stairs. Call it hindsight, if you like. I felt that once I went up that staircase I would be committed; that I would never escape.

From the top Aunt Ann looked back at me in surprise. 'Come on, Timandra!' she called. 'What's the matter, dear?'

'Nothing,' I said. Then I mounted the staircase and found myself in a dim upper corridor. Clearly someone didn't like light, or was economising.

Aunt Ann, maybe seeing my expression, sighed and laughed. 'This place ought to be a museum. Don't think there are many places in London like this. Maybe, being Americans, you'll find it interesting. Even Londoners find it strange. In many ways the place hasn't altered since the old people married more than fifty years ago. And of course it was old-fashioned then; it's been the Warwick family home since the mid-nineteenth century. Your grandfather was a fanatic in some ways; he hated changes. What a struggle we had to make him alter the plumbing, and as for that huge colour television set . . . But he enjoyed it really, though he pretended to be shocked by some of the improvements.'

'It is quite a place,' Tim murmured.

'Of course he was terribly mean, and he had no taste for real antiques or good modern furniture. Of course some of the things are well over a hundred years old, and there's quite a vogue for Victoriana these days. I hate it myself. Wait until you see our part of the house; it's quite different. In here, Timothy. Just leave the rest of the suitcases out here, Harry. The twins will sort out their things later.'

Tim disappeared into a room on the left, and I found myself in a big bedroom that struck very cold in spite of the small electric heater burning on the hearth. There was a huge brass bed covered with a rich, plum-coloured counterpane and more of the dark, heavy furniture.

'I hope you'll be comfortable,' Aunt Ann said anxiously. 'You'll have plenty of space, anyway. There's a big wardrobe – a closet, don't you say? – and a chest of drawers as well. The bathroom is at the end of the passage, on the left.'

She stood in the middle of the plum-coloured carpet, looking around. She was quite a handsome woman, though rather plump, but her face seemed to me to have no warmth. I thought her expression rather calculating, and I felt she didn't really care whether or not I was comfortable.

'If you want anything just ask me, or Nancy, of course,' she went on. 'But it will take the old thing a day or two to get used to you. She's upset because . . . Oh, well, it's been a difficult time, and, like the old man, she hates changes. I should just take your coat off, and wash quickly, and come down to dinner.'

'All right. Thank you.' I hardly knew what to say. We were in London, and tomorrow might be better, but I felt so terribly homesick and alien.

When I was alone I began to prowl around, looking at the pictures, the heavy glass bowls and silverware on the chest of drawers, the enormous wardrobe that smelled very musty. I searched for more light switches and found, with relief, that there was a light over the bed and another over a table. But the general effect was extremely gloomy, utterly different from my bright, pretty room in New York. I had thought I liked Victoriana, but enough was enough. I didn't think I was going to like *living* with it.

The curtains were plum-coloured and very thick. I

drew one aside and peered out of the window, but I could see nothing because of the fog. The silence was intense, and suddenly I felt so unhappy and scared that tears came into my eyes. Oh, we must have been crazy to come! We should have waited until summer and maybe stayed at a hotel with Uncle Serle and Aunt Esther. Even the thought of all there was to see in London did not comfort me then.

I made an effort to compose myself, because it would be awful to go down to dinner with red eyes. I took off my outdoor clothes and at once felt colder than ever. I was looking for the bathroom when Tim appeared. He smiled and beckoned. I looked into a room that was very like my own, except that the bedspread, curtains and carpet were of dark olive green.

'Oh, Tim!' I said shakily. 'It's all just awful. How shall we bear it?'

Tim looked surprised.

'I thought you'd be interested, Mandra. What's the matter?'

I stared at him in exasperation. We might be twins, but we weren't in the least alike in character. Tim was supposed to be the artistic, sensitive one, but he could be obtuse.

'The people, Tim. And it's all so *gloomy*.'

'It's gloomy all right,' he said cheerfully. 'Wait until you see the bathroom. The bathtub is a real period piece.'

'I'm going along there right now. We can talk later. If we don't hurry Nancy will put poison in the soup.'

Something in my tone seemed to arrest him, and he looked at me closely. 'You said that as if you really meant it. Don't be silly, Mandra.'

Maybe it *was* silly: just me being melodramatic because I was tired and homesick.

'She wasn't very polite, I admit,' Timothy went on.

'But I guess we upset her usual arrangements over dinner.'

'I think she feels we're usurpers. We've got most of the Warwick money, and she doesn't like it. Not that it's really any of her business,' I said, and I went quickly away along the corridor. The bathroom was certainly in keeping with the rest of the house, but the water was hot, which was some comfort.

When I emerged a few minutes later I was startled to come face to face with someone we hadn't seen before. She was a young girl, with bright fair hair and a pale, pretty face. She wore a very short, dark blue dress and a paler blue apron. For a moment she looked like an apparition from a different world – not at all the kind of person I expected to see at Victoria Lodge.

'Why, hello!' I gasped.

'Hello!' she replied, smiling. 'Look here, I'm sorry, but Nancy sent me to hurry you up. She's in an awful temper. It's not much of a welcome for you, is it? All the way from New York, and you get nagged because dinner's late.' She was eyeing me with friendly curiosity.

'I must just do something to my face, then I'll be right down,' I said. 'What's your name?'

'Margaret. They call me Maggie and it makes me furious. I've asked them not to, but they take no notice.' She sounded quite cheerful, however; as if nothing upset her very much. My low spirits rose slightly.

'Margaret is a much nicer name. You work here, then? Do you live in the house?'

'Yes,' she said, 'but not for long, if I have my way. My mother said I must live-in somewhere until I'm eighteen. She's old-fashioned, is my mother. My home's in a little village in Kent. When I said I wanted to work in London she was quite upset. She was in service herself before she was married, but it was a really good place. She worked for a famous actress in a lovely flat in Eaton Square. But the Warwicks pay me well; people will pay anything to get domestic help. Soon as I can I'm going to work in a big shop.'

'Well, it's very nice that you're here now,' I said warmly. 'Maybe you can tell me things.' I didn't exactly mean about the family, but she seemed to take it that way.

'I'm sure I can,' she said darkly. 'But not now.'

A gong made an impatient, booming sound below and she rushed away down a back staircase. Her bright hair seemed to make the scene less gloomy.

When I was ready I found Tim waiting in the corridor. He was examining a stuffed squirrel in a glass case. We went down the main staircase together and Uncle Basil was waiting for us in the hall.

'We're all having dinner together tonight,' he explained. 'Until the old man died we usually kept to our own part of the house, but lately we've come through more often. It's been lonely for Mother.'

The others were already gathered in the dining room. It was another huge room, overcrowded with furniture and inadequately heated. The long table was covered with a dazzlingly white cloth with an old-fashioned lace edging, and there was an impressive array of silver and glass. I was told to sit next to George, and he grinned at me.

'Come and join the family party! You must tell us all about New York. It sounds quite a place. You live in Greenwich Village, don't you? I thought only artists and foreigners lived there.'

'There are some others,' I answered quietly.

'You live in an apartment, I suppose? What they call a walk-up, I believe.'

'We live in a whole house. Uncle Serle has his office there, but otherwise . . .'

Nancy and Margaret arrived with the soup. Nancy went around in disapproving silence, and I looked at her doubtfully. She wasn't all that old, just the witch type. She was deft enough and moved quickly. When Margaret caught my eye she gave me a conspiratorial smile. She didn't seem overawed by the Warwick family, and her presence in the house was a curious comfort.

The meal progressed so slowly that I felt it would never end. I did my best to talk, but found it an effort. I couldn't forget that, yesterday evening, we had eaten dinner in the little courtyard behind the house on West 4th Street. It was rather a sooty little courtyard, overshadowed by a huge ailanthus tree, but I had always loved it and I had begged for a last meal outdoors. The night had been warm and starry, and now, so soon afterward, the chill, secret London fog hemmed us into the unfamiliar house.

The atmosphere around the table seemed to be full of tensions. I told myself that it was difficult for all of us, but I felt it was more than that. Our grandmother was the only one who seemed to behave naturally, yet at times she looked tired and remote, and she ate very little. Aunt Ann was jumpy and nervous, Uncle Basil was far too hearty, and George talked too much. But perhaps it was as well that he did, for his remarks covered what might have been uncomfortable silences.

Toward the end of the meal Tim asked a question about the London art museums and was met by blank stares.

'Well, I suppose there are plenty,' Aunt Ann said, after a moment. 'I was taken to the National Gallery as a child, but I haven't set foot in it since. I'm afraid that none of us is very interested in art.'

'Tim is going to be an artist,' I told them.

'Good heavens!' Uncle Basil exclaimed. 'How extraordinary! What gave you that idea, son?'

'With all that money he can have any ideas he likes,' said George. His father and mother frowned at him.

Grandmother said in a gentle voice: 'I used to like pictures as a girl, and even painted myself. People said I showed talent.'

'There are plenty of pictures in this house,' Uncle Basil said, helping himself to cheese. 'Relics of Victorian art by unimportant and forgotten painters. But of course people collect that kind of thing nowadays. Father had a valuer in a year or two ago. They wouldn't fetch a fortune, but there'd be a demand, astonishing as it may seem.'

Tim and I both knew that was true, but so many dark and unappealing paintings seemed oppressive.

'Do you think I can put this one away, out of sight?' I asked Tim thirty minutes later, when we were alone in my bedroom. After coffee in the drawing room, we had been released to unpack and go to bed early.

Tim stood with his head on one side, studying the painting of a Highland loch, with a group of shaggy cattle just visible in the grey-brown mist.

'Sure, why not? It's just ghastly.' He wandered across the room. 'And this one of the simpering lady with the dear little dog.'

'But it may hurt their feelings or something. Honestly, Tim, Nancy hates us already.'

'She doesn't seem very outgoing.' Tim admitted. He bent to unfasten the strap around my largest suitcase.

'Except toward the family, especially Uncle Basil. "I

hope the coffee is to your liking, Mr Basil, dear?" Oh, Tim, wasn't dinner awful? I know we shouldn't have come. They hate us because of the money. I guess it's natural, but it scares me.'

'That's silly!' said Tim shortly. 'They've plenty of money of their own. Well maybe not George. He did make one or two snide remarks, and Uncle Basil implied he wasn't too successful at his job. But you're tired, Mandra. Things will look better in the morning.'

'But there's such an awful atmosphere of strain,' I cried.

'Grandmother's kind of nice, though. I think she really is glad to meet us at last. I . . .'

'What was that?' I asked sharply, turning toward the door.

'Nothing. You're getting nervous.'

But I ran to the door and pulled it open. Nancy almost fell into the room. She recovered herself quickly and we stood eyeing each other.

'I was coming to see if you have everything you want, Miss,' she said.

'Yes, thank you, Nancy.'

'If you do want anything just ring the bell. Maggie'll answer it. Her legs are younger than mine, though heaven knows she's lazy enough. Thinks of nothing but her boy friend, and those noisy discos.'

I watched her walk away toward the back staircase, then I shut the door and faced Tim.

'She was listening at that huge, old-fashioned keyhole.'

'Just curious, I guess,' Tim said casually.

'But I don't like it. And there's no key in the door. I can't lock it.' I heard a faint hysterical note in my voice.

'You don't need to lock it, Mandra.' Tim sounded

amused. 'But, look, there is a bolt. Why don't you unpack what you need, then take a bath and go to bed?'

I followed his suggestion, but I was depressed to find that the water was only lukewarm. I returned shivering to my room and climbed into the big brass bed, leaving the heater glowing on the hearth. At least there were plenty of blankets, and – oh, joy! – my icy feet met something warm: a hot water bottle.

I lay in the faintly rosy gloom for a long time, unable to sleep. There was a grandfather clock in the hall, and I heard it strike eleven, then twelve. I had unpacked my flashlight, and once, guided by its clear beam, I opened my door and went softly along the corridor to the top of that great Victorian staircase. I could hear the clock ticking, but there was not another sound in the house. Outdoors it was equally silent; not even the noise of distant traffic.

I left the head of the staircase hurriedly, ashamed to realise that I found the old house eerie. It was cold, too; I was shivering again. I slept at last, but was haunted by bad dreams. I was running through the fog, chased by some unseen, unknown presence.

I awoke about four o'clock and remembered Norris Carey. He said he would call us, but maybe he would be too busy. Perhaps he had forgotten us as soon as he had left the airport.

If we had only one friend in London it would be a comfort. Someone from New York, who spoke the same language. I had liked him so much on short acquaintance.

The same language ... The Warwicks, Nancy and Harry spoke the same language, with some differences. But it was more than that. Norris knew our setting, and, for the moment at least, that seemed important.

One day, of course, I would like to make some British friends.

Norris *had* to call: he would call. I felt that he was a reliable person. I turned over and fell asleep again, and it was morning when I awoke.

CHAPTER 4

The Warwick Will

I was awakened by Margaret entering with a tray. She went to the window and drew back the heavy curtains, revealing dim grey daylight. I yawned and sat up.

'It's still foggy,' Margaret said cheerfully. 'But the sun will come out later. It was lovely and warm after lunch yesterday. I was out without a coat.'

I found that hard to believe. The fog pressing against the window looked cold and forbidding.

'Old Mrs Warwick doesn't get up until lunchtime,' Margaret went on, 'so Nancy said you'd both better have your breakfast in bed. Did you keep your fire on all night? I do sometimes, but they'd be terribly cross if they knew. You're used to central heating, I expect?'

'Yes,' I said. 'But the weather was still hot when I left New York. It must be awful here in real winter.'

'I wasn't here last winter, but I bet you're right,' she agreed. 'Central heating's common enough in England now, but old Mr Warwick wouldn't hear of having it put in. I heard him having an awful argument about it with Mr Basil. Nancy made tea for you, though I said I knew you'd rather have coffee.'

'Oh, tea will be nice, thank you. I often drink it.'

'Do you? I thought Americans drank nothing but coffee. I wish you'd tell me about New York some time.' Margaret prowled around, gazing at my clothes, folded over chairs. 'That's a very nice dress you were wearing last night. Would you mind terribly if I tried it on one day?'

'You can try on anything you like,' I said readily. I was going to need Margaret's company, though the Warwicks mightn't approve. 'But I'm taller than you.'

'Oh, dear!' she grumbled. 'There's Nancy calling "Maggie!" See you later.' And she hurried away.

Left alone, I eyed my breakfast tray. Bacon and egg, toast and marmalade, and a small glass of orange juice. The juice wasn't chilled, though they must have a refrigerator. There had been ice cream at dinner last night.

I was very hungry and it was a relief not to have to face another family meal. I made the most of the warmth and peace. The house was almost uncannily silent, and I decided to buy a transistor radio as soon as possible. I had left mine in New York.

I was up, washed and wearing trousers and a warm sweater when Timothy appeared. He also was dressed and he looked rested and cheerful. He said he had slept all night long. I didn't tell him about my troubled thoughts and bad dreams. He would have said I was silly.

We stood together by the window. By then the sun was struggling through the fog, but we could see only the lines of dark shrubs that marked the driveway, and tall trees closing the house in.

'The leaves are still green!' I cried, in surprise. I'd been feeling that it was almost winter.

'I can see a few just turning gold,' Tim remarked.

'They were all golden in New York,' I said.

'What do you say if we go out and look around the neighbourhood?' Tim was asking, when we heard a telephone bell in the distance. A few minutes later we heard footsteps in the corridor and Margaret knocked and looked around the half-open door.

'A Mr Burrell wants to speak to one of you. The telephone's in the hall, under the stained-glass window.'

'Burrell? Oh, the lawyer!' I cried. 'You speak to him, Tim.'

Tim was away for five minutes and I occupied the time in putting on my coat and tying a scarf over my hair.

'He wants to see us at three o'clock,' Tim said, when he came back. 'He sounded rather stiff and oldish, but very friendly. I said we'd be there. The office is in a street just off Chancery Lane. He says to take a taxi and the driver will know.'

'Taxi drivers here must be better than in New York,' I said. 'But we could look it up on the street map. I suppose we have to get it over, Tim.'

'I guess so. Just wait a second and I'll be ready.' And he went back to his own room.

When we ventured downstairs together I thought the house seemed brooding, dark and uncannily quiet. The only light in the big hall came through the stained-glass window on the right. We looked into the living room (the drawing room, they called it), and then into the dining room, thinking we ought to tell someone we were going out. Both rooms looked gloomy and were empty. Then Aunt Ann came briskly from the back of the hall. She wore a tweed skirt and a pink sweater.

'Oh, there you are!' she said brightly. 'Good morning. Your grandmother is still in bed, and Basil and George have gone off to work. Are you going out?'

'We thought we'd take a walk,' Tim said.

'Good idea. The sun's breaking through, and it isn't cold. You'll want to explore.'

'This afternoon we have to see Mr Burrell,' I explained, watching her closely.

'Oh, he telephoned, did he? Well, of course he wants to see you.' Her manner had stiffened perceptibly, but after a moment she managed a smile. 'Come and see our part of the house before you go out.'

She led the way along a side passage and through a door, then we were in a different, modern world. In the Basil Warwicks' part of the house there was white paint, contemporary wallpaper and furniture, and a great many well-arranged flowers. Aunt Ann showed us the living room, then the kitchen, which was cheerful with yellow paint. On one wall was a vivid modern print of an Italian scene, and a large refrigerator was humming gently.

'You should see the kitchens in the old part of the house,' she said. 'Though you never will if Nancy has any say in the matter. That's *their* domain.'

'This is just great!' I said. I would never have believed I'd be so glad to see a change from Victoriana, but the heavy, dismal atmosphere of the rest of the house had certainly been preying on my mind.

'This part of the building is much newer, of course. The house was damaged toward the end of the Second World War. Not badly, but the roof was unsafe. All the furniture was put in storage, and your grandfather and grandmother and the boys moved into a furnished flat for a time. When the repairs were done your grandfather had this part built on, with some idea of using the rooms as offices in connection with the family firm. They never were used that way, and when Basil and I married we took possession. Just come through when you want to. You'll find it dull with just your grandmother, and Nancy is being so cross.'

'I guess we'll be out a good deal,' I said quickly.

'Naturally. You're young and you'll want to enjoy yourselves in London. You've got the money, so why shouldn't you?' Her tone changed, growing sharper. 'Of course, things are mostly still tied up, with your grandfather dying so recently, but . . .'

She paused. Tim was staring at the print and didn't say anything. I said, after a moment: 'We're sorry if . . . the will seems kind of strange.' I felt very uneasy and awkward.

'We thought so,' she said. 'But the old man was certainly in his right mind four years ago, when he made it. That was when he learned about you from Dr Serle Dickson. There was no hope of contesting it. Now, if you'll excuse me, I've some telephoning to do. I haven't got much domestic help, and I'm always busy. There are all my committees . . .'

We retreated along the passage and back into the main house. We closed the front door behind us and stepped into the sun-touched fog.

'She does hate us,' I said.

Tim frowned. 'Hate is a strong word, Mandra. It sounds as if they were advised not to contest the will. I guess we'll learn more about it this afternoon.'

We walked a few yards, then turned to look at the house. It was certainly not beautiful, but it was impressive: a jumble of big windows, gables and enormous chimneypots. The new part was not visible from that angle.

'I don't think we can stay here, Tim,' I said, as we walked through the gateway and out into the quiet street lined with big trees – Plane Tree Walk.

Tim laughed and took my arm.

'We'll have to stay. How could we walk out? No one

will put poison in the soup, Mandra. Maybe it's kind of awkward, but that's all. We'll be out plenty. We needn't see them too much.'

'But the whole place gives me the shivers. It's cold, of course, but I don't mean that. It scares me.'

'Oh, forget it! We're going to get to know London, remember. Now isn't this pleasant?'

We had turned into a street called Duchess of Bedford's Walk. It was still misty, but the sky showed faintly blue and the air really wasn't cold. Big buildings stood back from the street and there were a great many trees. In the quietness we could hear birdsong. I began to feel happier.

Tim, who had been studying the street map, led us westward, and we were soon in Holland Park. In the mist the big sweeps of grass, the tall old trees, seemed to belong more to the country than to London. The only person in sight was a woman walking a dog.

We stopped to look at the long facade of Holland House and Tim said that he meant to draw it one day.

'Parts of it are Jacobean, the guide book says,' he explained. 'It was bombed in World War Two, but they've rebuilt this part very well. They have plays here in summer.'

We strolled on, seeing some peacocks and a deserted adventure playground. At the north end of the park there were woods and the air was suddenly so warm my winter coat seemed unnecessary.

'Oh, I do feel better now we're outdoors!' I cried. 'To think we're really in London, Tim – in the place that Father knew. Let me tell you something. I can't imagine him being a child in that awful house. No wonder he didn't tell us much about it.'

Later, by chance, we found Church Walk off Holland

Street, and we were enchanted by the sunlit charm of the little old shops, with their gay canopies and bright paint. Tim grew absorbed in some art books in a small bookshop, and I found an antique shop with some prints of old London in the window.

After so much peace, Kensington High Street was a surprise. There were big stores, crowds of hurrying people and endless traffic. I loved the red London buses.

'London's so big,' I remarked, as we walked back to Victoria Lodge. 'I wonder if we shall ever see it all?'

'Not if you don't want to stay,' Tim said, and I frowned. The shadow of Victoria Lodge was already falling over my spirit again, but maybe I *was* being silly.

'We'll have to stay for a while, I guess.'

'We said three months, but I'd like to go over to Paris for a couple of weeks,' Tim said yearningly. 'When I've seen all the art museums here.'

'Uncle Serle suggested three months. But we don't have to stick to it,' I pointed out.

'Well, wait and see, Mandra.' Tim was beginning to sound irritated. 'We only arrived yesterday. Forget the Warwicks and that darned house. I want to get to know London real well.'

'OK, I want to know it, too.' Tim would always slide out of things, I thought. Even as a little boy he had retreated into a secret world of drawing and painting, and, though he'd always had friends, no relationship had ever gone very deep. Mother died when we were five, so maybe we were too young to understand our feelings, but the difference between us had been painfully apparent to me when Father died. Tim minded desperately; I know he did. But he had his retreat and he disappeared into it. *I* had no comfort until the worst of the pain faded, and I learned to be contented and happy again with the Dicksons.

Tim just wasn't going to see anything difficult or unpleasant, and I foresaw that I was soon to lose him to the art museums of London.

We did take a taxi into the part they called the City of London, though I would have liked to go there in one of the big red buses. By then the sun was shining brilliantly and it was very warm. On the way we saw Hyde Park, Green Park, Piccadilly Circus and Trafalgar Square. It was very exciting, and I even forgot to be nervous at the thought of the coming interview with Mr Burrell.

The building where Burrell, Gordon and Gray had their offices was built of dark stone, and it was tucked away down a tiny, secret street full of shadows. It looked as if it had been there for hundreds of years and I expected a small, musty office, with a very old gentleman sitting behind an old-fashioned desk.

But the waiting-room was large and pleasant, and the office into which we were led after five minutes or so was quite modern and, being high, was filled with sunlight.

Mr Burrell's hair was turning white, but he looked very healthy and brisk, as if he might enjoy a good game of golf. He greeted us in a friendly way and asked how we liked London.

Tim replied that we hadn't seen very much yet, but it looked just fine. He added that he was keen to see the art museums as soon as possible.

Mr Burrell was interested and asked a lot of questions. Maybe I was wrong; he certainly couldn't be totally addicted to golf, for he knew quite a lot about art and gave Tim the names of several small collections not in our guide books. When he learned that Tim planned to be an artist he was even more interested.

'Well,' he said, 'perhaps I can give you some advice if you plan to stay in London. I have friends who could help with art courses or teachers. How are things at Victoria Lodge?'

Tim laughed and looked at me. I didn't know what to say.

'Bit of a shock, was it?' Mr Burrell asked. 'It's an archaic place. I've been there a few times. Still, you may find that you settle down, and I think your grandmother would be glad. It would give her an interest. Of course nothing can be done about the house until she dies, and she may live for several years, though I understand her health is poor. I suppose, then, you'd want to sell Victoria Lodge?'

'I guess so,' I answered fervently, and he looked at me shrewdly, but made no comment.

'There's Victoria Cottage, too,' he went on. 'That's the house near Henley; not a cottage, really. It's an attractive property, though rather neglected. Old Mr Warwick was very mean, I'm afraid. He hated to spend anything on improvements. Your grandmother used to be very fond of Victoria Cottage. It's shut up, at the moment, but those two old family servants go down there occasionally to clean and air the place. You'll have to go and see it.'

I sat tensely on the edge of my chair.

'We . . . It all seems so strange,' I ventured. 'Our grandfather leaving everything to us.'

'Not quite everything. There's an annuity for your grandmother, and the Cheams get five thousand pounds each. Various people who worked for your grandfather get two thousand pounds. Capital transfer tax will be heavy, but when everything is settled there should be a considerable sum left, as well as an interest in the family business. With the capital well invested you should both be sure of a reasonable income.' He went into some details that I found difficult to follow. I wasn't really trying to listen, for only one thing seemed important. When he paused I asked hesitantly:

'But didn't Uncle Basil and George get anything?'

Mr Burrell moved some papers around on his desk.

'Unfortunately, no,' he admitted. 'It's an unusual will, in many ways, but perfectly legal and valid. There's no need for you to worry about it.'

'But did they . . . did they resent it very much?' I persisted. I felt awful, but I wanted to know. I felt I did know.

Mr Burrell's shrewd gaze came back to my face.

'Didn't they welcome you? They all seemed most anxious for you to visit London.'

'I guess so, but . . .' I avoided Timothy's eyes.

'It was a surprise to them all, of course,' Mr Burrell said. 'It's perhaps unfortunate that Basil Warwick and his son were passed over. Basil Warwick had some idea of contesting the will, but we advised him not to, and he seemed quite resigned. We don't handle his affairs, but I believe him to be a man in a good position, certainly not short of money. So I shouldn't worry.'

He rose, smiling; his manner was very firm. The subject was closed. 'I'll keep in touch with you both. There'll be papers to sign . . . various developments as time goes on. Meanwhile, when you want money . . .' And he named a Kensington bank where we would be able to draw reasonable sums.

Escorting us to the door, he added: 'I'm sure things

will settle down as you get to know the family. Mr Warwick has told me that they want to go on living in their part of the house for the time being, and this will be quite in order as long as old Mrs Warwick is alive. Enjoy London!'

'We didn't find out much,' I said, fifteen minutes later, when we had found our way to the great square called Lincoln's Inn Fields. 'He didn't want to talk about that will.'

We were sitting on a seat under trees, with sparrows hopping around our feet.

'Maybe there's nothing more to find out,' said Tim. 'He told us not to worry, and I'm not planning to.'

'But I'm sure there's something we haven't been told. Did you hear what Uncle Basil said in the car last night? Something about being cut off with fifty pence.'

'Sure,' Tim agreed. 'That's a British saying. It means he inherited nothing.'

'No. To be cut off with a shilling is the right way to say it, and that's what he said at first. The British changed their currency, and there's a table in my guide book. It's a reprint of an old one. A shilling became *five* pence. But he said fifty, in a very bitter voice.'

'Oh, Mandra, forget it!' Tim was growing irritated again. 'You have too much imagination.'

'No one ever said so before,' I retorted. 'Oh, well, where's the street map? Let's walk back to Trafalgar Square and take a first look at the National Gallery.' I knew it was no good pursuing the subject, but I did feel there was something we hadn't been told.

While I was in my room, about half-an-hour before dinner, the light bulb over my bed gave a loud pop and went out. It wasn't quite dark outside, but my room, facing north, was always gloomy, and I certainly needed every light on. If I didn't get another bulb, I couldn't read in bed, and I'd bought a couple of paperbacks for that very purpose. I didn't want another sleepless night, but I was determined to have something to read.

So, how to get another bulb? The only way seemed to be to brave the kitchen and the Cheams. I hated the very thought, but I wasn't going to suffer just because I was a coward. So I went along the dimly-lit corridor to the back stairs and quietly descended into even deeper gloom. I was wearing rubber-soled sandals and my feet made no sound at all. The passages that led to the kitchen quarters were illuminated with only two widely-spaced low-power bulbs. The floor was stone and there were various doors that might open on storerooms. I could hear voices in the distance and brighter light spilled through a partly-open door at the end. As words reached me, I stopped abruptly.

'They went to see the lawyers.' It was Nancy's voice, harsh and angry-sounding.

'They had to.' I recognised Harry's voice. 'They're the heirs. That's why they've come.'

'Well, they shouldn't be. That's what I think, and what you think, too. It's downright wicked that poor Mr Basil and Mr George got nothing. Old Mr Warwick never liked Mr George, not even when he was a boy. And he was a nice enough lad. Always polite. I rocked 'im in 'is cradle.'

'Lazy, that's what Mr George was. The old man couldn't stand laziness. You know that well enough, Nance.'

'Well, what did poor Mr Basil ever do but start 'is own business? It's the insult I mind, and 'e minds. The wickedness of it, to say in the will: "I leave my son Basil the sum of fifty pence, because that is all he is worth".'

Harry gave a cackle of laughter. 'You shouldn't listen at doors, Nance. You'll be found out one day.'

I stood frozen to the spot. So that was it! And it *was* an insult – a derisive voice from the grave. Nancy wasn't the only one who listened at doors. I'd have to retreat, without the bulb.

I nearly jumped out of my skin when a hand touched my arm. It was Margaret.

'They were talking about the will,' I whispered. 'I don't usually listen, but I came for another bulb.'

'I'll get you one. They're in here,' she whispered back, opening a cupboard door near us. 'The will – Nancy's always talking about it. I know all about that. But I'll have to go, or she'll be yelling for me.'

She thrust a bulb into my hand and sped away toward the partly-opened door. I turned and went slowly back up the stairs. I removed the old bulb and successfully fitted the new one, then I went to the window. The fog was gathering around the house again.

A voice from the grave. Oh, how deeply Uncle Basil must have resented those words in his father's will!

I shivered, once more oppressed by the silence and gloom of Victoria Lodge. I wanted to understand about the will, but I wished I hadn't listened outside the kitchen door. I knew that those terse, mocking words would haunt me, as they probably haunted Uncle Basil.

CHAPTER 5

Interlude At Hampton Court

Dinner was a quiet meal, eaten alone with our grandmother. She mainly talked about the past and did not seem to be much interested in our New York background. If she referred to Father it was generally with a remark about his youth.

Afterward we were invited into the other part of the house for coffee, and we found Uncle Basil, Aunt Ann and George in the brilliantly-lighted living room. At least it was warm in there and looked more cheerful.

George, it seemed, was going out. He drank his coffee quickly and rose, smoothing his hair.

'Well, excuse me, everyone. Got "a date",' he said. Then he looked at me, and his eyes seemed to show a mixture of speculation and admiration. 'Why don't we go out together one evening, Cousin Timandra? How would you like that?'

Not at all, I thought, as Uncle Basil laughed.

'That's a good idea, isn't it, Timandra?' he said. 'You don't want to go everywhere with your brother.'

I forced myself to say politely that it would be very nice; but I hoped George would soon forget the idea. I didn't like him, yet I was, at the same time, vaguely sorry for him. I thought he probably didn't have much of a life, in spite of his overdone cheerfulness.

When George had gone we watched television. That was a relief, as we didn't have to talk, but I didn't think much of the programme – apparently a popular British comedy series. Father had kept his British voice, but he had learned to use American terms and phrases before we were born. I still found so many strange words rather bewildering.

Occasionally I glanced at Uncle Basil. He was sitting slumped in his chair, and, in repose, he looked older – a man with many worries. Yet, I wondered, why was he worried, when he was doing well in business, had a large car, a pleasant home and a good-looking and efficient wife? Maybe he hadn't yet recovered from his father's death and the unfriendly will. Unfriendly was really a mild word to describe it. Grandfather must have disliked Uncle Basil very much to insult him from the grave.

Aunt Ann seemed restless. She was sewing and only glanced at the television occasionally, but she kept on changing her position and she was tapping one foot in an irritated movement.

Tim, I saw, was not paying attention to the programme either. He seemed lost in thought, but they were probably happy thoughts because he was smiling faintly. I suddenly felt very lonely, and, when I thought of Norris Carey, I was startled at how much I wanted to see him again. But probably he would never call me. Why should he, really, when we were only chance acquaintances?

As soon as I could tactfully do so, I excused myself and went to my room. There I wrote a long letter to Uncle Serle and Aunt Esther and a shorter one to Bill. Bill would want to know how I was getting on, but I was fairly sure that he would have another girl by the time I went home. The thought made me a little sad, but maybe only because I was already so homesick. It had been a pleasant friendship. Norris . . . But I mustn't think about him. One couldn't fall in love in just a few hours. At least, I had never believed it possible until then.

In both letters I stressed the pleasure of seeing London and I tried hard to make Victoria Lodge sound amusing. Uncle Serle and Aunt Esther would only worry if they knew the true state of affairs. But I ended my letter to them: 'I think we may be home for Christmas. London is just fine, but we haven't much in common with the Warwicks. It would be so much nicer if you were both here, too.'

The next morning I found Timothy in the bathroom, sketching the remarkable bath.

'I'm going to do a series of drawings,' he told me. 'I might try writing a short article to go with them. I bet some American magazine would be interested.'

'Maybe they would,' I said, exasperated by his self-absorption. 'I wrote to Uncle Serle and Aunt Esther last night, and I told them we'd be home before Christmas.'

Tim looked up from his drawing.

'Well, we might be, but that's far off yet.'

'*Too* far off. Tim . . .'

'I don't know why you find everyone so sinister,' he said. 'You let Nancy and the whole atmosphere get you down.'

'But I told you about that fifty pence insult,' I said. 'Don't you feel that they all – except Grandmother – hate us?'

'I think it's just that they aren't our kind,' my brother said slowly. 'Uncle Basil can't have been very pleased, but he's trying to be nice to us. I guess I find George the worst. I'd never get to be really friendly with him.

Grandmother's kind of sweet, but I admit she worries me. She's vague ... Sometimes I wonder if she remembers who we are.'

'She's old,' I said. I certainly found her the least worrying member of the household.

'Not so old, really. She's only seventy-four.'

That seemed like Methuselah to me.

'Nancy and Harry really scare me,' I confessed.

'Oh, Mandra!' Tim was growing annoyed. 'You sure have too much imagination. They'll come around. My famous charm will do the trick before long.'

'You flatter yourself, my boy. I guess it won't. Nancy only cares about her dear Mr Basil. And, of course, her dear Mr George. But Harry scares me the most.'

Tim said that Harry wasn't a very attractive person, but why worry? He did his work and that was all that mattered. So I said no more, but my fear and dislike of Harry Cheam remained. He was ten years younger than Nancy, a little wizened man, with sharp features and a sharp glance. I had the feeling that he missed nothing. He was a quiet man, hardly ever speaking, but I was aware of his presence.

On our second day in London Timothy and I separated, after a visit to the bank in Kensington. Tim went off to the Tate Gallery, and I walked in Kensington Gardens. The sun shone warmly and suddenly I was much happier. I saw Kensington Palace and the Peter Pan statue, and watched the children playing with sailing boats on the Round Pond. Away from Victoria Lodge I did not feel lonely. It was good to be getting to know London.

I had lunch in a restaurant, then I spent most of the afternoon in the big department stores. I bought two cashmere sweaters and a really warm bathrobe, a necessity in the icy atmosphere of Victoria Lodge. In the golden sunlight of late afternoon I walked in Holland Park before returning to Victoria Lodge.

Margaret met me in the hall.

'Oh, you've been shopping!' she cried. 'Will you show me what you bought? Later, I mean. An American telephoned: a Mr Norris Carey. He sounded awfully nice. I said you'd be in this evening.'

I went upstairs almost on wings. For once that Victorian staircase didn't oppress me at all. Not even the sombre atmosphere of the house, as the October brightness faded into the usual fog, could affect my spirits. Norris had called me after all!

As I changed into one of the new sweaters I waited for the phone to ring. When I heard it I was just ready, so I rushed down the staircase. Nancy had been before me, however.

She turned to me with a sharp: 'It's for you, Miss. Comes to something when I have to run my feet off answering calls for visitors. And just at dinner-time, too. It's a Mr Carey.'

When I heard Norris's voice all the shadows, all my vague fears, were forgotten. He wanted me to go to Hampton Court with him the next day.

'And your brother as well, of course, if he's free,' Norris said.

Timothy was passing just then, so I asked him. It was a relief when he said: 'No thank you, Mandra. I'm planning to see the Wallace Collection and then maybe the Courtauld one.'

So it was arranged that I should meet Norris at Waterloo Station the next morning.

'I guess it will be safer if we go by train,' Norris said. 'I plan to rent a car when I go out of London, but I kind of feel the traffic here would be too much to cope with.'

So he was leaving London! That was the only cloud in my sky during dinner. But I told myself not to look ahead, or no further into the future than the next day. The knowledge that I was going to explore Hampton Court Palace with Norris Carey was enough to get me through the gloomy meal and the two hours of television that followed it.

No invitation had come from Uncle Basil and Aunt Ann, and I was glad. There was a ballet programme that I enjoyed, though I didn't think Grandmother was paying much attention. Most of the time she lay back in her chair with her eyes closed. She looked sick and as if she had little hold on life. Old age seemed very sad and I didn't like living with it. But Norris was young . . . I let my thoughts drift to coming pleasures.

I resolved not to talk to Norris about the people at Victoria Lodge and my unformed fears. I was rather ashamed of my feelings. Tim thought I was silly and maybe he was right. I didn't want Norris Carey, who, after all, didn't know me well, to think me over-imaginative or neurotic.

I ventured on to the London buses and I reached Waterloo Station triumphantly five minutes before the time Norris had said. But he was already there waiting for me. My heart leaped with joy at the sight of him. He looked an unashamed American tourist, with a camera over his shoulder and a map in his hand. He really was very good-looking, even more handsome than I had thought on the plane. But more important than that, he was somehow so clearly a nice, intelligent person.

As the train carried us out of London I thought: I am

in England. I am on an English railway train with Norris Carey. And then I caught his glance and for some reason we both laughed. Oh, I felt really happy, then.

I found I had to tell him a little about Victoria Lodge and the Warwicks, because he remembered what I had said on the plane and asked some questions. I tried to make it all sound amusing, as I had done in my letters to New York, but he seemed to read more into my words than I had intended.

'It doesn't sound very cheerful,' he said, frowning. 'And I guess they can't like it much that you and your brother inherited the money.'

'Oh, a funeral parlour would be more cheerful than Victoria Lodge,' I agreed, still trying to speak lightly. 'You'll have to come and visit us. But I warn you that Nancy may put poison in your soup.'

'She sounds just awful!'

I shouldn't have said that, I knew.

'She's a witch, for sure. Maybe she keeps a cauldron in those old-fashioned kitchens.' I wished we could get off the subject.

'And your cousin: George? What's he like?'

'He wants us to go out together one evening,' I said.

'Well, I suppose that would be natural,' Norris remarked. He glanced at me thoughtfully. 'Don't you like him?'

'Not much. And I don't really think he likes Tim and me any more than the Cheams and his parents do.' I'd gone so far I couldn't help adding: 'He probably needs the money more than Uncle Basil and Aunt Ann do. I feel badly about that. He doesn't seem to have much of a job, selling cars.'

'You may be wrong about his feelings for you,' Norris said slowly. 'You are . . . very attractive, Timandra.'

That made me feel a warm glow of pleasure, but suddenly I pictured George's face and remembered the hurried, eager way he had left us that evening we went in for coffee.

'Do you know,' I said, 'I think he has a girl already . . . one he cares about. Oh, he hasn't said so, but I kind of have a feeling.'

After that the subject was changed, and we didn't mention the Warwicks again during that long, lovely day. By the time we left the train the morning had turned sunny and hot, with a glorious blue sky. We strolled by the Thames under the October trees. Some were still green, but others were turning gold or deep russet. Then we sat on a seat to read our guide books.

After lunch at an hotel we made our way to Hampton Court Palace, and I was enchanted by the ancient buildings, the quiet courtyards and the overpowering feeling of history. People like Cardinal Wolsey and Henry the Eighth began to seem real to me, and I took great joy in all the beautiful furnishings and pictures.

Later we walked in the gardens. There were flowers everywhere – Michaelmas daisies, dahlias and roses still in great profusion. There were not many people around as it was a weekday, and I wandered beside Norris in a peaceful dream.

We entered the famous maze, with its high hedges, and we sat on a seat in the centre for a long time, enjoying the warmth of the sun and each other's company.

'I'm very glad we met on that plane,' Norris said, as we rose to leave at last. 'We must go someplace else very soon. You haven't seen the Tower, or St Paul's or Hampstead Heath . . .'

'Or Westminster Abbey, or the Houses of Parliament,

or Buckingham Palace,' I added. 'I haven't really seen *anything* yet. And there are all the antique shops . . .'

'Yes, we must look around for those. Chelsea, maybe, or Shepherds Market.' Then Norris glanced at me. 'That is, if you'd like to.'

'Yes, please,' I answered, and we both laughed.

We had difficulty in finding our way out of the maze, so it seemed quite natural when Norris took my hand. He continued to hold it as we walked to the railway station.

Oh, I didn't want the day to end. The shadow of Victoria Lodge was falling over my spirits by the time we arrived at Waterloo. But I cheered up again when Norris said he would take me all the way home. We sat on the top of a bus and commented on the passing scene.

Dusk was falling as we walked through the quiet Kensington streets, and the fog was beginning to wreathe around the street lights.

'Is it always foggy in London in winter?' I asked, and Norris laughed.

'Winter! Think of those roses and the hot sun. Oh, I guess not. We just seem to have struck a patch. It comes up every evening.'

When I turned into the driveway that led to Victoria Lodge Norris seemed surprised. For a few moments the trees and dark shrubs hemmed us in; then he saw the house. It was still light enough for it to be clearly visible – the turret, the gables – the fog only faintly blurring the outlines of the heavy Victorian chimneypots.

'Is *this* the place?' He stepped back and stared in astonishment. 'Pure Gothic!'

Darkness seemed to be falling fast by then. Even as we stood staring at the house it seemed to recede into the gloom.

'You should see the Victorian staircase,' I said, conscious that I was dreading the parting, dreading going indoors. 'Would you like to come in now?'

'Another time,' he said quickly. 'Goodbye, Timandra. I'll call you tomorrow. I'll wait here until you're indoors.'

I had been given keys to both doors; they were always kept locked. The first heavy door always stuck a little. I gave it a push. When the second one opened the big hallway was dimly revealed in the one light that was on near the staircase.

I looked out into the gathering fog, but could not see Norris at all. I waved, in case he was still standing there, then I was back in Victoria Lodge, with the world shut out.

Tension stiffened the back of my neck. I thought of all the people under that roof, silent in the dark house. I jumped violently when a harsh voice said: 'Dinner in ten minutes. You've kept it late again. Not very considerate, I'd say!'

Nancy was somewhere in the shadows of the kitchen passage. Another light flashed on and the staircase showed more clearly. I ran up it and into my room. The day at Hampton Court seemed already unreal. *This* was reality, however unpleasant. I knew that I hated Victoria Lodge. Maybe it was irrational. Nancy, after all, was old. But there had been venom in her tone.

CHAPTER 6

What Happened Near Henley

A whole week passed. I began to feel that I knew London quite well, and I knew that Tim felt the same. He was absorbed in the art collections and his own work. He had made a number of drawings as he sat on seats in the parks and squares. He said he found Londoners easy to talk to, and he had made friends with an art student who had been copying a painting in the National Gallery. They sometimes met for meals or to go to the cinema.

During that week Norris and I had spent several more days together. We had explored the Tower of London, wandered in the old grey streets around Covent Garden and in many of the beautiful parks. We had seen famous buildings and churches and browsed in antique markets and little shops. It was lovely to have money to spend and I bought several things, all Victorian. Even my dislike of Victoria Lodge had not really dampened my interest in the period.

One evening we went to the Royal Opera House to see the Royal Ballet dance *The Sleeping Beauty*. Maybe that was the happiest time of all. I liked Norris more every day, and it alarmed me to realise how much I was depending on his company. He had already visited two great printing works near London, and later he was going up north, to Liverpool, Glasgow and Edinburgh.

As long as Norris was in London I felt fairly safe, but I was scared of being left alone again. I felt convinced that, when that happened, the atmosphere of Victoria Lodge would really close in. For things had not improved. The house still seemed dark, brooding and filled with tension. Neither Nancy nor Harry had ever shown the faintest lessening of their veiled – or not so veiled – dislike. There were times when Grandmother seemed better and would talk quite animatedly, but much more often she looked dreadfully vague, unhappy and sick. Clearly she had not got over Grandfather's death, and even our presence did not seem to mean much to her.

During that week Tim and I didn't see much of Uncle Basil and Aunt Ann, though George came occasionally to talk for a while. Once he walked through into the main part of the house just as Norris arrived to take me out, and he didn't seem very pleased.

'I thought you knew no one in London,' he said to me later. His tone was almost accusing. I did try very hard to be nice to George, but it was sometimes difficult. My friendship with Norris was nothing to do with him.

'Norris is just visiting. He won't be here for long,' I said, and the words made my heart sink. Without Norris . . .

'Well, don't forget that you're coming out with me one evening,' George said quickly. 'Maybe a film . . . a *movie*. And dinner somewhere where there's music.'

I answered vaguely. It was the last thing I wanted.

When I asked Norris what he had thought of George he laughed and said: 'Not my type. But he is a bit pathetic. Do you really think he has a girl?'

'Sure to have,' I answered confidently. 'He isn't the kind to be without. He doesn't seem to work very hard. I wonder why he doesn't get a proper job. It needn't be with his father.'

'The house is all you said,' Norris went on. 'That old

woman who opened the door might well put poison in the soup.'

'That's why I haven't asked you to dinner yet,' I told him. 'The least she'd do would be to pour the soup down your neck.'

I was still trying to keep it light. Norris knew me better now, but there was really nothing concrete to tell him, only my vague fears.

I always returned to Victoria Lodge with dread, and was perfectly conscious of the relief of shutting the front door behind me when I went out. I had definitely made up my mind that I wouldn't stay there for long, whatever Tim might decide. Either I would move into a hotel or go home to New York. It would be sad to leave London while there was still so much to see, but I could return one day. Once the business was finished and Mr Burrell thought it all right to go . . .

But when Tim and I went to see Mr Burrell again, to sign some papers, he seemed to assume that we were happy and settled at Victoria Lodge. I tried to get the words out, but I didn't manage to say anything. After all, there was nothing definite. Later I asked myself why I should really care that an old woman, who probably wasn't quite right in the head, bore a violent resentment against us because Uncle Basil had been insulted and passed over in his father's will. Uncle Basil was always perfectly pleasant when we saw him. Why should I really mind at all when Harry Cheam looked at me in a way that was difficult to explain? Speculation, doubt, dislike? All three, maybe. But of what importance was Harry Cheam?

If only Nancy hadn't continued to hover. More than once I had found her right outside my bedroom door. Sometimes I knew she was lurking in the shadows when I was talking to Norris on the phone.

Margaret was the only one in the whole household with whom I felt at ease. It was a relief to talk to someone young, lively and thoroughly human. I liked to hear tales of her boy friends, her home in the country, and her adventures when trying to collect the autographs of her favourite pop singers. Even Margaret's attitude to the Warwicks and the Cheams was a comfort. She somehow made the lurking tensions seem less real, or at least less important.

It was Margaret who told me that Harry and Nancy were not as devoted to each other as I had assumed.

'Devoted!' she said scornfully. 'They fight like cats! And, if you ask me, they always have. Oh, I admit there are times when they really gang up together. But you should hear Harry go for old Nancy . . . Sometimes it quite scares me.' For once her pretty, carefree face looked sober. 'The other day he called her a blooming old witch who should be burned at the stake, and he looked as if he'd like to do the burning himself. She does give him an awful life, you know. She really is an old devil. She's always blaming me for things I haven't done. This morning she fell over a bucket she'd left there herself, but she yelled at me.'

'I don't know why you stay,' I said.

'One day I'll just walk out. But I promised my mother I'd stay until my birthday, and it does suit me to be here in a way. As I told you, my boy friend works in Kensington High Street, and I can easily slip out to see him.'

The next morning I had an accident. Tim had already gone out, but I was later than usual. I was still in my room when I heard Nancy calling from downstairs: 'Telephone, Miss!'

I had not heard the phone ring, but then I had just had my head in the wardrobe. I rushed out of the room toward the stairs. The upper corridors were always rather dark, even in broad daylight, and I didn't see the mop that had fallen across the top of the staircase.

I tripped, staggered and felt myself falling headlong. The dark red carpet seemed to surge up to meet me and I grabbed wildly at the broad hand-rail. Somehow, at the expense of a badly-wrenched elbow and wrist, I managed to stop my fall, but I landed with a painful clatter against the thick wooden banisters.

From somewhere at the back of the hall Nancy's cross old voice cried: 'What're you doing? Breaking your neck?'

Feeling dazed and shaken, I straightened myself and glanced upward to see what had caused my fall. The mop had now swivelled around and the head was pointing toward me.

'I fell over the mop,' I said breathlessly, as I continued down the staircase. 'It was right across the top.'

'It's that young Maggie,' said Nancy. 'I'll tell 'er she's a careless girl. A fine thing if you *had* broken your neck!' and she disappeared.

I went to the phone and lifted the receiver, which was lying on the table. But there was no one on the line.

'What's the matter, Timandra?' Aunt Ann came into the hall from the side passage and looked curiously at me. I was still holding the receiver, and, even in the dim light, she could evidently see I was upset.

'Nancy said there was someone on the phone and I nearly fell down the staircase,' I told her. 'Someone has left a mop right across the top step. And there's no one on the phone now.'

'Oh, dear! How very careless. You look quite shaken.'

She seemed genuinely concerned. 'Come on through and have some coffee. I had my breakfast early, so I was just going to have some.'

I accompanied her into the other part of the house. I needed the coffee, though it wasn't very long since I had eaten breakfast. My arm was aching and I still felt badly shaken.

Of course, I thought, it must have been Margaret: she was young, and a bit careless, and it had just been an accident. But when Aunt Ann sent for Margaret she came, looking indignant, and flatly denied she had left the mop anywhere near the top of the staircase.

'I left it in the bathroom,' she said. 'I was going to wash the floor, but Nancy called me down again to finish in the kitchen.'

Nancy had insisted on being present as well. 'You're a liar, my girl!' she said sharply. 'I nearly broke my own neck yesterday when I fell over a bucket you'd left in the hall.'

'You left it there yourself,' said Margaret. Her lower lip was unsteady and she looked very young and defenceless. 'I'm not a liar. My mother brought me up properly, and if she knew . . .'

I felt terrible for Margaret's sake, and by then my arm was throbbing fiercely. I clasped it with my other hand and said unhappily: 'Oh, let's forget it. I didn't kill myself.'

'No,' said Aunt Ann. 'But you've hurt your arm. Shall I call the doctor?'

'I've only wrenched it,' I said quickly. '*Please!*'

So Aunt Ann let them go. I drank my coffee and went back into the dark hall. And there was Margaret, still upset.

'It wasn't me, honestly,' she whispered. 'I think Nancy

must be failing. She's often forgetful. Or else she did it on purpose. Sometimes I think she hates you enough to kill you.'

I laughed, and after a moment Margaret laughed, too. She couldn't really believe that Nancy Cheam was capable of murder.

'I'm OK. Forget it, I don't blame you,' I said. But, after that, I walked very carefully, for I was haunted by the memory of those moments when I was in danger of a possibly fatal fall.

When I met Norris later in the day, by previous arrangement, he said he had not called me that morning. I did not explain why I had asked – at least not the fact that the call had caused me to fall. I knew that once I started to talk about my uneasy suspicions I would say too much. After all, it might have been Mr Burrell, though surely he would have called again later.

Norris had a dinner engagement with a business acquaintance of his father, so I was back in time to speak to Tim before our meal. I told him the whole tale, and he was concerned, but rather annoyed.

'Don't be a fool, Mandra!' he cried. 'You can't really believe that Nancy would do a thing like that on purpose?'

'I guess she just might,' I said slowly.

'But that's nuts, as you know quite well. She's a cross old thing, but that doesn't mean . . .'

'Then who was on the phone?' I demanded. 'If anyone was. It wasn't Norris, and no one else has called again since. The more I think . . .'

'Didn't you ask Nancy who it was?' Tim queried.

'No. At first I was kind of dazed and upset, and then . . . I was scared to speak to her again.'

'Then I'll ask her, if it will make you feel any easier.'

'Sure, you ask her,' I agreed. 'She's probably right outside, listening at the keyhole again.'

We were in Timothy's room and he looked startled.

'Oh, Mandra, you *are* getting jumpy!'

'Go and have a look,' I said.

I followed Tim to the door. When he opened it there was Nancy, a few feet away along the corridor, dusting the glass case that held the stuffed squirrel. It seemed a strange hour of the day to be dusting.

Tim went to speak to her, and I partly closed the door and stood shivering with cold and nerves.

'She says it was a man,' Tim explained, when he returned. 'She thought it was your American friend, but he didn't speak very clearly, so she called you. Probably a wrong number. Do buck up, Mandra!'

'Well, it could have been a wrong number,' I admitted. 'But she was out there, Tim.'

Uncle Basil and Aunt Ann came through for dinner that evening and during the meal the house near Henley was mentioned.

'You really ought to go and see it,' said Uncle Basil. 'After all, it will be yours one day. It's an attractive place and the roses may still be out, though of course the garden is rather neglected. There are two rowing boats. Ever done any rowing?'

'Oh, sure,' Tim said eagerly. 'We often rent rowboats on the lake in Central Park. And we have friends on Long Island who have boats.'

'George said something about driving out that way,' Aunt Ann remarked. 'There's some man who lives at Stonor, in the Chiltern Hills, who is interested in buying a car. Maybe he could take you to Victoria Cottage on the way, and pick you up later.'

'Oh, please don't bother,' I said hastily, but Tim frowned at me. I knew he was keen on the idea of rowing, but surely there was some other way of going? I didn't want to drive there with George.

But the next evening George offered a definite invitation. 'I'm going to the Chilterns tomorrow,' he said. 'So why don't you both come along? I took the car out there today, but the chap couldn't make up his mind, the old ditherer. I didn't ask you to go with me today, because I went unexpectedly. He called up the place where I work. Victoria Cottage ought to be OK, aired and so on, because Harry drove Nancy out there today. Routine check. Funny that, wasn't it? All three of us out that way, but I didn't know until I came back.'

Harry sometimes drove the big old car that had belonged to Grandfather. In fact, part of his job had once been to act as chauffeur.

Tim and I exchanged glances. I knew that Norris was engaged the next day, and Tim had no definite plans. Tim wanted to go, and it seemed unreasonable to refuse.

'Do come,' George said, quite eagerly. 'I'll be glad of company.'

When he spoke like that he seemed quite nice. I nodded.

'We'll be glad to go,' Tim said. 'I might make some drawings of the house, and we can try out the rowboats.'

'Well, George won't be with us all the time,' I said later. 'And we'll see the English countryside.'

The weather had been rather wet for a day or two, but when we set off for Victoria Cottage it was warm and sunny again. The car was a big one and very new, and

George drove it well. He was wearing a rather startling blue and green shirt and his long hair was smooth and sleek.

'I can't drive very fast,' he explained ruefully. 'Running it in, you know. And it's more than my life's worth to damage it. I only hope the chap will buy.'

After that he didn't talk much for quite a long time, for the traffic was heavy. But at last the suburbs were left behind and there were signs of the real country.

'I'm taking you through the hills,' George explained, as he headed for West Wycombe. 'It's a bit longer, but I thought you'd like it. Must show you England.'

He was obviously doing his best to be pleasant, and I was enchanted with the long village street of West Wycombe and the church and mausoleum on the hill. After that the Chiltern Hills rose on either side in all their glowing autumn beauty. The beechwoods were turning russet and gold here and there and, in some of the lower fields, the chalky earth had been ploughed into folds. Other fields were still yellow with stubble, and there were a lot of wild flowers. I began to feel happy. It was always good to be away from Victoria Lodge.

We swung off the main road and the car began to climb. We drove over a common bright with bracken, then swept down off the top of the ridge into a valley that was so lovely in its gentle symmetry that I cried out with pleasure. And Tim exclaimed over the old brick and flint cottages, the inn and ancient church at Fingest.

'The church is probably nine hundred years old,' said George. 'And some of the cottages and manor houses have been here for several hundred years, I suppose. I'm not very keen on period architecture. I'm a city boy through and through, but even there I'd rather see modern buildings and not old churches. I like a lot of people around, too. The country would give me the creeps. Oh, it's pretty, all right . . . You could always come again.'

I began to think that I'd like to, very much, and I could see Tim felt the same. We were city people, too, but that gentle Chiltern country was putting a spell on us.

We drove down the beautiful, serene Hambleden Valley and reached the Thames at Mill End. Soon after that George turned the car down a narrow lane, then through a wide gateway on to a curving drive. The driveway, overgrown with grass and neglected, was bordered with rhododendrons and dark box hedges.

George stopped the car when Victoria Cottage suddenly came into view. It was long and low and built of brick and flint, with gables and a roof of russet tiles. It was not old as the many houses we had seen had been old (later we saw the date 1840 over the porch), but it was charming. The garden all around the house dreamed in the October sunshine. It certainly was rather neglected, but there were still roses of every hue. They were past their best, but flowering bravely, as if winter would never come.

It was nothing like Victoria Lodge. There was no menace, no gloom.

'It's lovely!' I cried. 'Oh, Tim, if it's ever ours I don't think I shall want to sell it. We could keep it as our English country cottage.' Then, when I saw George's expression, I wished I hadn't been so tactless. He had said he didn't like the country, he probably didn't want Victoria Cottage, but my words had reminded him of our inheritance. It really was terribly unfair that he had been left nothing.

'I'm sorry,' I said contritely and thereby probably made things worse. It might have been better to ignore the fact that George minded.

'You're lucky, aren't you?' he said laconically. 'The money and the possibility of two houses as well. Not that I want either Victoria Lodge or this place, but they'll sell for very high prices. If you do want to sell Victoria Cottage some day you'll get a small fortune for it. People go for houses on the river.'

'But where is the river?' Tim asked. 'We haven't seen it yet.'

'Around the back, at the bottom of the garden. Well, I'll leave you,' George said quickly. 'You've got the keys? And don't forget your picnic lunch. Leave a little food for me, though if I have time I'll have a bite in Henley. If he's keeping the car we'll have to get back as best we can, you realise that?'

'We don't mind,' Tim assured him, as he reached for the basket that held the food, bottles of bitter lemon and a flask of coffee. 'But won't you get stuck up in the hills?'

'No. This chap has another car and a chauffeur. I'll beg a lift back to Henley, at least. We can go back by bus and train.' He turned the car and was gone. It was a relief.

'You sure said the wrong thing,' said Tim.

'I know. I could have bitten my tongue off. Things were going pretty well until then,' I said. 'But I shan't want to sell it. Where shall we go first, Tim?'

'Let's look at the house, then we can eat lunch outdoors. It's quite warm enough. I'm hungry, though it's only twelve o'clock.'

We walked slowly toward the house. A little to one side there was a herbaceous border, still glowing with late dahlias, golden rod and Michaelmas daisies. The quiet air smelled delicious. It was a heavenly place!

The front door was painted white and half hidden by a bower of fading climbing roses, but we could just see the date up above. I pushed one of the labelled keys into the lock and the door swung open. Tim followed me in.

The house struck very cold, but it seemed clean enough and better cared for than the garden. The contents were shabby, with faded curtains and covers on the chairs, but there was no heavy Victorian furniture. The place was furnished like a cottage, very simply. We wandered from room to room, pulling back curtains and letting the sun shine in. From the back windows we could see a gently sloping lawn, and then the shining waters of the Thames, with woods and hills on the other side.

There were some narrow, dark passages near the kitchen, and the kitchen itself had been modernised, with an electric stove, a refrigerator (not working) and even an electric percolator standing on a white-painted table. Tim had turned on lights as we went around, and he tried the taps over the sink. Water gushed out. We had even seen a telephone in the hallway.

'Everything seems in working order,' he said. 'Shall I switch on the refrigerator and put the bitter lemon in?'

'No, we can't wait for it to get cold,' I answered. 'I'll drink it warm, for once. Oh, Tim, I've kind of fallen in love with this house. It would be fine if it was lived in a little. Why don't we come and stay here for a night or two soon? I wonder if they'd let us?'

'Can't stop us, I guess,' said my brother.

'It isn't ours yet, remember. It belongs to Grandmother. But I *would* like to stay here. We could camp in a corner. We can look upstairs later. Don't you want lunch?'

We ate out on the terrace, facing the river. The sun was hot and I sighed contentedly. If Norris had been there, I thought fleetingly, it would have been quite perfect.

'It's just great to be so far away from Victoria Lodge,' I murmured. 'The evil spell doesn't extend this far.'

Tim looked annoyed.

'Mandra, you do say the darnedest things! Evil spell!'

'I can't help it, Tim. I hate the atmosphere in London more every day. Well, if you've had enough to eat, let's go and look for the boat.'

'In the boathouse, George said.' And Tim rose, stretching his slender body. We walked down to the river bank, through grass that was rather long and full of weeds, and looked at the swiftly flowing river.

'There's some current, and it looks deep,' Tim said. 'Different from the lake in Central Park.'

'Yeah, but we've rowed on the sea, remember. We'll be OK.' I was full of confidence.

There were two rowing boats, apparently in good condition. Tim began to tug at the one nearest the water.

'I suppose it's all right,' he said, with unusual caution. 'The water is running fast, Mandra. The boat looks OK, but it's fairly old.'

I began to grow impatient, for I longed to be out on that shining river. I lent my weight to pushing the boat into the water.

'Of course it's OK, Tim. George said he'd been out rowing only a month ago. He brought some friends down here. Hang on to that rope. We don't want to lose the boat before we get in. The oars are on board. Let's go!' And I jumped in.

Timothy rowed first, and I sat trailing my fingers in the water. The bank beyond the garden of Victoria Cottage was hung with what I thought were willows, and there wasn't another person in sight. It was idyllic.

Tim pulled the boat into the middle of the river and began to row downstream. I sat placidly, enjoying the heat of the sun on my shoulders. I was wearing an almost new jacket and trousers and I took off my jacket. The blouse underneath was sleeveless.

'Can you believe it will soon be winter, Tim?' I asked. 'I can't, though that evening we arrived I thought England would always be cold and foggy.'

'It's darned hot!' said Tim. 'I'm glad I left my jacket at the house.'

'Don't forget my turn,' I said. 'I row just as well as you do,' and then I gave a startled cry. 'Tim, we're taking in water!'

The idyllic feeling had gone in a flash. The river was swift and deep, and we were some distance from either bank.

'Can't be,' Tim said, rowing steadily. 'I splashed a bit when I was getting started.'

'But we are!' I cried, on a rising note of terror. 'It's bubbling up through this board under my feet. And under you as well. *Tim!*'

Timothy glanced over his shoulder and stopped rowing. 'Gee, you're right!'

'It's coming in faster every second. You'd better make for the bank, or we . . .'

Tim looked at both banks. The ones that were level with us were quite high, and, where there were no bushes and brambles, they were sheer and probably slippery.

'Guess we'd never get up there,' he said, calmly enough. 'Hang on, Mandra. I'll turn around and row back.'

'You'll never make it. It's *spurting* up!'

Tim's feet, and mine, were already ankle-deep in water, and it was deepening every second. He swung the boat around with some difficulty against the current and began to row with all his strength toward the nearest place where the bank was low and overhung with willow trees.

'It would be no good if we landed on the other bank,' he panted. 'How'd we get across?'

'There might not be a bridge for miles,' I agreed. 'Oh, Tim, do hurry! Shall I take one oar?'

'No, don't try and move,' he said. 'I'll do my best, but I think we'll have to swim for it.'

CHAPTER 7

Accident Or Design?

The boat went through the water more and more slowly. Now we could see Victoria Cottage again, but it was still some distance away. The boat was filling so rapidly that I knew it couldn't be long before it sank. Tim was right: we'd have to swim.

When the boat was still a hundred feet or so from the bank there was an ominous gurgling sound and it began to settle in the water. I stood up resignedly. I was no longer all that scared, but I didn't look forward to it.

'OK, we'll have to swim,' I said. 'I hope the water isn't too cold.'

We took to the water as the boat disappeared beneath the surface of the Thames. We had to swim only a short distance before it was shallow enough to stand up, but the thought flashed through my mind that, if we had been non-swimmers, we would certainly have drowned. Tim seized a branch of willow, and held out a hand to me. Somehow we scrambled up the bank. I nearly lost one sodden shoe and shrieked, but I still had them on when we reached the field above. That was luck, because the field was muddy and churned up by the hooves of cattle. Because we were spending the day in the country I had put on sensible shoes. If we'd had to swim much further I would have had to kick them off, of course.

'We made it!' said Tim, gasping.

'But isn't it awful? We've lost the boat and we're both

soaking wet! Tim,' I said softly, glancing around, 'are those animals all right?'

Tim gazed at the cows. I had to admit they looked peaceful enough, but suddenly I wasn't so keen on the English countryside.

'I guess so, Mandra. But move carefully. It isn't far to go. I can see the lane near the house.'

'And our own gate,' I added. I walked cautiously across the field, keeping my eye on the cows. I hoped they were all cows . . . maybe there was a bull among them. Our shoes squelched at every step, and everything I wore was soaking wet. I'd lost my nice new jacket in the river, but at least Tim would have one.

'How shall we manage, Tim?' I asked. My voice was a bit shaky. I felt cold suddenly and very uncomfortable. 'What if we have to go back to London by bus and train?'

'I don't know,' Tim admitted. 'Ugh! It isn't as warm as I thought.'

We were walking rapidly up the drive to Victoria Cottage when we heard a car behind us, and there was George. His face behind the windscreen looked heavy and sullen, but his expression quickly changed to a look of sheer amazement. He leaned out of the window.

'Hey!' he called. 'What have you two been doing? You're soaking wet!'

'We sure are,' I agreed, relieved to see the car. At least we were spared public transport. 'The boat filled with water and sank. We had to swim for it.'

George drove past us and parked the car on the gravel near the front door. He got out as we approached.

'Good heavens!' he exclaimed. 'Both boats were all right a month ago. Lucky you can swim!'

'Isn't it?' I said. My voice must have sounded strange, for I saw Timothy glance at me.

'There are clothes in the house,' George said quickly. 'I keep a few things here. You're thinner than I am, Tim, but they'll fit well enough. Trousers . . . a sweater. As for Timandra, Grandmother used to be here quite a lot. There may be something . . .'

'Thanks,' I said. 'But I guess Grandmother's clothes won't do for me. Trousers and a sweater will be fine, if you have enough clothes here.'

George nodded and we entered Victoria Cottage. Tim asked tentatively: 'You didn't sell the car?'

George stopped in the hallway and the sullen, defeated look returned to his face. I suddenly felt terribly sorry for him.

'No,' he told us. 'He says he's almost certain he'll buy it, and he'll let me know in two days' time. The chauffeur will come and fetch it. I'll believe it when he comes, with a cheque. It's a rotten life! Well, you'd better come with me and I'll find you the clothes.'

He gave us towels and what clothes he could find. It was wonderful to peel off my wet things and rub myself dry until my cold flesh tingled. The trousers fitted well enough. The sweater was rather large, but that didn't matter. The problem was shoes. There was a pair of sandals for Tim, but nothing for me. Even Grandmother had left no shoes. George found a pair of thick socks and those had to do.

I hobbled across the gravel and climbed into the back of the car, while George locked up the house and the boathouse.

'You both ought to have a hot drink,' he said, when he came back.

'I'm afraid we drank all the coffee,' I explained.

'Well, there'll be a place on the road.'

I sat in silence as George drove along the main road

toward Marlow. When he pulled up at a café by the roadside I protested: 'I can't go in without shoes!'

'Who'd care?' Tim asked. 'Well, OK: we'll go in, and I'll bring you something.'

He returned in a minute or two carrying a cup of steaming tea. 'It'll warm you up, Mandra,' he said. Then he looked at me closely. 'What's the matter? You look kind of strange. It was an awful thing to happen, but we came out of it all right. So . . .'

'I'll tell you later,' I said. I wasn't ready to talk about my frightening thoughts.

Tim let it go at that, and, when we drove on, George seemed in better spirits. Apparently he had convinced himself that the car was as good as sold.

'It's a pity you lost the boat,' he said. 'I wonder if there's any hope of getting it up. Did it go into deep water?'

'Pretty deep,' Tim answered. 'We know where it went down, but maybe the current will move it.'

'It's possible. Still, you're rich enough to buy another boat next year, if you're still in Britain. I don't know why it should sink like that. Did you examine it before you took it out?'

'Not really. Mandra was in a hurry, and you'd said both boats were fine.'

'Well, I thought they were,' George said. 'Naturally. To think you might have been drowned.' He sounded genuinely horrified.

'Not us, I guess,' Tim said easily. 'We swim like fishes. But the banks were so high I tried to get back to where we started. The other side would have been no good, because there didn't seem to be a bridge.'

'You could have crossed at Hambleden Lock.'

'We didn't know that.'

After that we drove back to London almost in silence. When we entered Victoria Lodge with our arms full of wet clothes Nancy was in the hall.

'Back early, aren't you?' she demanded. 'Why, what's been happening?'

'The twins had an accident,' George explained. 'The boat sank and they had to swim for it. If the water's hot, Nance, they'd better have baths.'

'It's hot if Maggie hasn't run it all off, Mr George,' Nancy said. She disappeared into the kitchen regions without another word.

Thirty minutes later Tim came to my room. I had had a bath and dressed and was brushing my hair. I could see in the mirror that my face was grim and thoughtful. I *felt* grim. I didn't like my thoughts at all.

'Now, Mandra, what is it?' Tim asked. 'It was a pity we got wet, but there was no real harm done. As George says, we can buy another boat.'

'Oh, Tim!' Exasperated, I put down the brush. He never would see things, admit anything.

'I suppose you mean,' he said, 'that you think someone damaged the boat deliberately?'

'Well, it does seem mighty strange to me that a boat that was quite all right a month ago should sink so quickly. Someone must have done something to it. Wrenched the boards apart, maybe, then put them back so that they looked OK. Or maybe bored holes. We should have made sure that someone brought up the boat and examined it.'

'We were too wet to do anything then, and there was no one to ask.' Timothy stared at me. 'We couldn't have asked George to go fishing for a boat, and he had nothing to do it with. Besides, he was upset about the car.'

'George was there yesterday,' I pointed out.

'Not at the house. He just went to that place in the hills.'

'So he said. But he could have stopped at Victoria Cottage. It wouldn't have taken ten minutes to damage the boat.' I paused, then went on: 'Uncle Basil and Aunt Ann told him we wanted to see the cottage: they probably said we were keen on rowing. If we hadn't gone with George today, we'd have gone some other way. And no one knew we could swim, because we didn't mention it.'

Tim walked around the room. 'Mandra! You can't accuse Cousin George of trying to drown us!'

It did sound awful and unlikely, but I was no longer the trusting Timandra of New York.

'Do you think I like having such thoughts?' I asked desperately. 'I feel terrible about it, Tim. But George needs money. He isn't very successful at selling cars. He might feel . . .'

'It's only in books that people murder for the sake of money,' Tim began heatedly, but I shook my head.

'Oh, don't be a fool, Tim! You know perfectly well that murder is done every day for seven dollars and fifty cents. Only,' I added sadly, 'I don't think it was always the case before. It's done for less – for nothing. Just because people feel violent.'

'But you're suggesting calculated murder,' Timothy pointed out. 'And how do we know George would get the money if we were dead?'

'We don't know,' I admitted. 'But maybe George does. It's something we haven't been told. We haven't made wills, have we?'

'You know we haven't. Mr Burrell didn't mention it. Maybe we can't until we're twenty-one. I don't know much about the law, especially over here, but I guess the money is tied up until then.'

'Maybe, if we died,' I said slowly, 'it would go to the next of kin. That's usual, I think, especially if people haven't made wills. And the Warwicks are our next of kin. There's no one else.'

'But, Mandra, even if that's true . . .' Tim looked very unhappy.

'Of course,' I said, starting to brush my hair again, 'Nancy and Harry were down at Victoria Cottage, too. And they heard that conversation about the rowing boats. Nancy was serving dinner and Harry had come into the dining room to do something to the hot plate. It wasn't working properly, remember? So they both heard. Harry could have damaged the boat, and even Nancy could have, I guess. She's little and old, but she's very strong. I've seen her moving heavy furniture as if it weighed nothing.'

'For heavens sake!' Tim exclaimed. 'What would *they* get out of it if we died?'

'No money, I suppose. It could be just hate because Uncle Basil and George were passed over in the will. They make no secret of the fact that they're devoted to them. And if we'd both drowned it would have looked exactly like an accident.'

'There would have been an inquest. They'd have got the boat up and examined it.'

'Maybe whoever did it wasn't thinking that far. Or maybe the job was done so well it would look just like the boards had rotted.' The more I talked the more likely it sounded. I was shaking, but my right hand continued to brush. 'When it had been under water for a time . . . Oh, I'm terribly afraid it was George. When I nearly fell down the staircase I thought it was Nancy, but even that could have been George. I remember now: when I was having coffee with Aunt Ann she mentioned that George had gone out late. He could have been in our part of the house and found the mop in the bathroom. He'd know I was still in my room, because I had my little radio on until just before it all happened. Then, when he left the house, he could have called up, disguising his voice so that Nancy . . .'

'Mandra, do stop!' Tim seized my arm. 'Accidents happen to people every day.'

'Oh, sure,' I agreed. 'But, Tim, soon as I can I'm going to find out what happens to the money if we die.'

'We aren't going to die. Take it easy, Mandra.'

I turned to face my brother. 'No, we're not, Tim, because we're going to be very careful from now on. Let's get away from this house! From all the people in it as well. Let's move to a hotel, or take an apartment . . .'

'I don't see how we can,' Tim said slowly. 'And even if you're right – and, mind, I think you're being silly – it would look too suspicious if we both died. No one would risk it.'

'Well, maybe George isn't quite sane. We know Nancy isn't. George wants money,' I insisted. I was remembering something Margaret had said. Margaret always chattered when we happened to be alone together. 'Tim, Margaret said George asked his father for money and was refused. Margaret goes through to help Aunt Ann sometimes, and the other evening they had friends in to play bridge. Margaret was in their kitchen before the guests arrived and she heard George and Uncle Basil having a row.'

'Margaret shouldn't have listened or told you about it,' Tim said.

'Well, she did, but I forgot to tell you. She said they were shouting and Aunt Ann went in to shut them up. George wanted five hundred pounds. That's not much for Uncle Basil, is it?'

'Maybe Uncle Basil feels that George should earn his own money.' Tim was sounding really cross and fed up. 'You shouldn't let Margaret gossip, Mandra.'

'Maybe not, but we're family and we have to know what's going on in this awful house.' Suddenly I felt I'd talked enough. It was clear I wasn't getting through to Tim . . . my own brother, my twin, who had been like part of myself when we were little. The sombre room, the big dark house all around us, the mysterious people with their probably dark thoughts . . . Oh, I hated it all and was scared. I burst into violent tears.

I hardly ever cried, but it was all too much. It had been a long and upsetting day. Suddenly I longed for Norris. I would have given almost anything to be with him, eating dinner in some peaceful, civilised place. When I saw Norris again I would tell him everything. I would have to risk him thinking me silly and imaginative. At least his sane, unbiased viewpoint would be some help.

Tim seemed shocked and startled by my tears. He put his arm around me. 'Don't, Mandra! I didn't mean to be unkind. Only I didn't want to encourage you in all those wild thoughts. The Warwicks do seem pretty strange sometimes, and I bet they do resent that will, but it's probably no more than that. We'll think about renting a furnished apartment, if you feel so strongly about it. It'll probably hurt their feelings, but . . .'

'I don't care!' I sobbed. 'I'm going home to New York before Christmas, anyway, but until then . . . Yes, please, Tim, let's be on our own.'

'I may be staying over here,' Tim said. 'I might study art in London or Paris after Christmas. You'll have to do what you like, Mandra. You – you want to be where Norris Carey is, don't you? And he'll be going back.'

I stopped crying and mopped my eyes. I felt shamed and shy, because Tim knew how I felt. 'It isn't only that,' I said quaveringly. 'I do like Norris, Tim, and he'll be going back long before Christmas. I don't know how much he likes me, though.'

'Pretty much, I guess,' said Tim. His calm assurance was some comfort.

CHAPTER 8

More Danger

I was admitting to myself by then that I loved Norris Carey. The warmth and rapture that I felt when in his company was undoubtedly the real thing – something I had never felt before. It was wonderful that the often alarming time in London should be illuminated in that way, but there was terror in my heart as well. Because it might not be real for Norris. He might regard it simply as a holiday friendship and he was going home at the beginning of November. Before that he would be away from London for several days.

We had had such wonderful times. We had strolled on Hampstead Heath and visited Ken Wood House; we had sat on Primrose Hill in the October sunshine, and got to know Regent's Park and the Zoo; we had been to Madame Tussaud's and to a concert at the Royal Festival Hall. Sometimes we had walked hand in hand, laughing and exchanging our knowledge of British history. Norris had seemed happy; I was sure he liked me. But he had never hinted that it was more than that and that he would want to see me again in New York.

Of course we had not known each other very long, but that day on the plane already seemed a whole lifetime away. So much had happened since then. I had had so many experiences of both happiness and fear that I felt a different girl from the one who had left Manhattan.

On the day after the affair at Victoria Cottage Norris

and I met again. We decided to go back to Westminster Abbey, for we had only been once and there was so much to see. After a while we went through the door into the cloisters, and, as we strolled around, Norris asked:

'What's the matter, Timandra? You look kind of worried.'

So the moment had come. I was glad, and scared, and I stammered as I started to speak.

'N-Norris, will you listen? There *is* something. I am terribly worried, but Tim says I'm silly and over-imaginative. I have to tell someone else. I have to know what you think.'

He walked more slowly and said quietly: 'Of course I'll listen. You should have told me before. It's to do with the Warwicks, isn't it? And that – that awful house?'

'The worst thing only happened yesterday,' I said shakily. 'You see, it's like this . . . I always hated that house. From the moment I walked up that Victorian staircase . . .' And then I told it all, as calmly and carefully as I could. As I talked I could hear that there was nothing really concrete in the tale. But Norris seemed to take it seriously. His face was very grave.

'It would be so convenient for them if we died,' I ended.

Norris had been holding my hand all the time, and now his grip tightened.

'Yes, it would. I should go to see the lawyer and ask him what does happen to the money. It would at least set your mind at rest if you found that none of them would get any if you and your brother died. I can see that these incidents have scared you, and the whole atmosphere of the house, but it's quite true that there's nothing really definite. Tim's right when he says that it would look too suspicious if anything happened to you both. But I don't like it, especially the boat incident. You would both have drowned if you hadn't been such good swimmers. You said no one knew you could swim.'

'I guess a lot of New Yorkers can't swim,' I said, much relieved that I had been taken so seriously. A weight seemed to have rolled off my heart. Norris had not laughed. Of course, in a way, it made the danger more real, but for the moment that didn't trouble me.

'But,' Norris went on, 'I think you should try to forget it until you've spoken to the lawyer. There may be nothing in it, Timandra. Let's go and look at the little cloister again. I kind of like that place. It's so small and peaceful.'

We walked through the dark stone passageway and came out in the tiny, silent cloister, where sunlight lay across the garden.

'Timandra,' Norris said suddenly, 'I know I told you to forget it, but do be careful until I come back to London.'

I jumped with surprise.

'But you're not going to Liverpool until Sunday night, are you?' I asked, trying to hide my deep dismay.

'It's all changed,' he said ruefully. 'I'm going north tomorrow. I'm spending the weekend in Liverpool, then going on to Edinburgh on Monday night after a few hours in Glasgow. I'm going by train, because it's quicker than driving. Maybe I'll rent a car when I get back. I feel more confident about the traffic now. Look, I'll call you the minute I get back to London.'

Then he turned me toward him and kissed me, warmly and slowly. Suddenly, so close to him, I was so happy I was not worried about anything. It was only later that the thought of losing him hit me.

When we drew apart I looked up at him and laughed

rather tremulously. 'Maybe it's against British law to kiss in Westminster Abbey.'

'There was no one to see.' Norris glanced at all the quiet doorways around the courtyard. 'And I've been wanting to do that for quite a time. Let's go for a walk by the river.'

I would have walked anywhere with him. I felt warm and justified and real. We crossed Westminster Bridge and strolled along the South Bank toward the Royal Festival Hall. My fears were not mentioned again, and I did not even remember them until we had parted. The parting was bad enough; I did not know how I should manage to exist without him for several days.

At Victoria Lodge that night I was divided between joy at the memory of that kiss and unhappiness because he was going away. Liverpool was only two hundred miles from London – about the same distance as Washington was from New York – but Edinburgh was in Scotland, much further away. I could only hope that the days would pass quickly.

The next morning I called the office of Burrell, Gordon and Gray from a phone box, but I was told that Mr Burrell would be away until Monday, or possibly Tuesday. The girl asked if it was important. If so, perhaps I would like to speak to Mr Gordon instead?

I said I would wait until Mr Burrell returned, but I left the phone box feeling unsettled. I'd have been glad to know, yet I couldn't face a strange lawyer.

On Saturday George asked me to have dinner with him and then go to see a film. I couldn't think of an excuse quickly enough, and George said: 'That's settled, then. We'll have a good time.'

I didn't look forward to the outing, but during dinner at a small Italian restaurant George was a pleasant enough companion. He asked a lot of questions about New York and I did my best to amuse and interest him, but it was a strain. I kept on thinking of Norris and wishing I were with him instead. So I was glad when we were settled in the cinema and there was no more need to talk.

After a time George tried to take my hand, then put his arm around me. I don't say I actually had to beat him off, but I had to indicate pretty clearly that I didn't like it. Out of the corner of my eye I saw that he looked surprised and rueful. Probably he was used to being a success with girls.

The very next morning I saw him out with a girl. I was taking a solitary walk before lunch, and, as I strolled along Holland Street, there was George and the girl just disappearing down Church Walk. I hurried to the corner and looked after them. She was young and very slim and her hair was pale gold. Suddenly she looked up at George, laughing, and the glimpse of her profile showed me that she was extremely pretty in a soft and gentle way.

George bent toward her and took her hand, and it was so clear that there was intimacy between them that I was puzzled. George loved that girl, so why had he bothered with me? Well, I told myself, his parents might have told him he ought to be polite to his American cousin, but he'd tried to be a lot more than polite. It would surely have been natural if he'd explained that there was someone else.

I puzzled about it all through the grey, cold day, which seemed to last forever. I missed the sunshine and I longed for Norris. Grandmother was not very well and had stayed in bed, so Tim and I had lunch alone. Aunt Ann said afterward: 'You should have come to us. I did mean to ask you, but I'm afraid I forgot.'

'We were all right,' Tim said cheerfully, while I just stared at Aunt Ann. She looked even more tense and anxious than usual. Something must be worrying her very much, I thought.

That afternoon Tim and I took a brisk walk through Hyde Park, then we walked along Piccadilly to Piccadilly Circus, where we had tea in a hotel. It was something to do, and even Tim didn't want to sit drawing in the cold wind.

Fast-falling darkness didn't improve my spirits and Sunday supper was a dreary meal. Afterward we watched television and read and I was glad when bedtime came.

The water was rarely hot enough for Tim and me to have baths one after the other, so we had fallen into the habit of testing it first and then deciding which of us should have one in the morning.

'It's pretty chilly,' I reported, after a trip to the bathroom.

'Well, I guess it's your turn,' Tim said, and I groaned.

'Why don't we toss for it? You are mean, Tim! A cold bath will just about finish this awful day.'

Tim tossed a coin and I lost. I gathered up my things and went to run the water. While I waited for the bath to fill I gazed around me. It really was the most fantastic bathroom. The bath must have been there for a hundred years. It was enormous, with huge brass taps; the outside was mottled marble and it stood on intricately carved feet. The toilet, on a little platform, was of blue-and-white patterned china with an ancient wooden seat, and the cabinet on the wall would have delighted an antique dealer's heart. As for the walls themselves, they had once been pale green, but had turned a dirty white in most places, peeling and unattractive.

The water was hotter than I had expected and I sighed with relief. Even when I ran the tap again it was still quite reasonably warm, so it was nice to sink down into the bath. That was the really great thing about it: you could lie almost flat and still have room to spare.

But, having started to look around with observant eyes, I couldn't stop. The place was clean enough, but I thought nostalgically of the bathroom Tim and I shared at home in New York. It had a beautiful blue bath, with a matching wash-basin, curtains in scarlet and blue, and a bathmat with a design of fishes. Here . . . Oh, why didn't someone think of getting the painters in? Soon the walls would start falling down. The plaster *had* fallen in a lot of places.

My eyes travelled downward to the level of the rim of the enormous old bath. It was fitted to the wall and there was a kind of handle, in a slight alcove, that one could use to heave oneself out of the water. And behind the handle the plaster had deteriorated very badly.

I sat up a little, for I had seen something that didn't look right. Behind the handle some of the plaster had fallen away to show wires . . . electric wires? They looked old and one was protruding a trifle. Uncle Basil had said once that the whole house needed rewiring. He had said something about suspecting there would be trouble if something wasn't done. In fact, he had said he would have a word with Mr Burrell about it, as Grandmother wasn't capable of dealing with such matters any more.

If you touched electric wires with a wet hand . . . I shrank back into the water, shivering violently. The water wasn't hot any more, but it wasn't that which caused the shivers. It was the sight of those dangerous, menacing wires.

I got myself out of the water somehow, keeping well away from the handle. I let the water out, dried myself and put on pyjamas and a bathrobe. Then I felt more able to look closely at what had happened behind the handle. Where the plaster had fallen away the edges looked quite new, raw, but there was no plaster lying on the rim of the bath, and there had been none actually in it when I turned on the taps.

I went quickly along to Tim's room and found him still fully dressed, sitting on his bed with some art books spread around him. He looked startled when he saw me.

'What is it, Mandra? You're white as a sheet!'

'Tim, come and look at the bathroom!' I cried urgently.

'What, for heaven's sake?' But he came at once, though walking calmly, unhurriedly. I showed him the exposed wires and explained how I had noticed them in time.

'You know what would have happened, Tim, if I'd put my wet hand against them?'

By then Tim was pale himself. The wires looked dangerous enough to upset anyone.

'Oh, Mandra!' he said. 'No wonder you look upset! The plaster's fallen in a lot of places, but *that* spot would have been fatal.'

'But someone must have moved the plaster,' I pointed out. 'There was none when I turned on the taps. So why didn't they notice where it had come from? It seems mighty . . . strange.'

'Something the matter?' asked Uncle Basil's voice, and he was looking around the half-open door. He stared in surprise at our grave faces. 'What is it? I just slipped in to see if Mother's asleep.'

'Yes, she is. I've looked at her several times,' I told him.

'Oh, well, you know how it is. Ann gave me no peace until I checked she was all right. We'll ask the doctor to come if she isn't better tomorrow. She's had these turns ever since Father died. But what's upsetting you both?' I pointed at the wires. 'But good heavens! They're completely exposed. That's really dangerous!'

'Yes, I might have been electrocuted if I hadn't seen them in time, before I got out of the bath,' I said, watching him closely.

'How terrible! But what did I tell you about this house? I did mention the wiring to Burrell, and now I'll have to insist that the job is done at once. The whole place must be properly inspected, then I'm afraid it will be a big job. I suppose the plaster fell out and . . .'

'But Mandra says there was no plaster in the bath,' Tim told him. 'So someone should have noticed when they moved it.'

There was the sound of footsteps out in the corridor and we turned to see Margaret. She had been out for the evening and was making her way toward the stairs that led up to the attic, where she slept. She looked pretty and cheerful, but her expression altered when she saw us.

'Come here, Margaret,' Uncle Basil ordered. 'Miss Timandra nearly got herself electrocuted while she was having her bath. Did you clean in here today?'

'How awful!' Margaret gasped. 'Well, Mr Basil, I never clean much on a Sunday. I just dusted a bit and wiped the bath.'

'And did you notice these exposed wires?'

Margaret peered at them, growing pale. She shook her head.

'Was there any plaster lying in the bath?'

'Oh, no, I'm sure there wasn't.'

'It must have been all right when I had my bath this

morning,' Tim remarked. 'I often use that handle because the bath is so deep. If I'd put my hand there when . . .'

I shuddered and Uncle Basil said quickly: 'Well, I don't understand it, but very luckily there's no harm done. I'll try and cover the wires until I can get the job done properly, and, in the meantime, no one is to use the bath. Mother is the only other person who uses this bath, so you or Nancy must warn her first thing in the morning, Margaret. Not that she'll be getting up early, if at all. Where's Nancy now? Do you know?'

'In the kitchen, I suppose.' Margaret sounded as if she had no wish to know.

'Well, will you go and ask her to bring Miss Timandra a hot drink, please? What will you have, my dear? Milk?'

'Nothing, thank you,' I said. 'I'm going to bed.' I didn't want to see Nancy or anyone else, but Tim followed me into my room. He shut the door behind him, and I climbed into bed, still shivering.

'Oh, Tim, I'm so scared!' I cried. 'It can't have been just an accident.'

'It certainly is mighty strange,' Tim agreed, frowning.

'We *have* to get out of here!'

'Maybe you're right,' my brother agreed. 'We'll find an apartment for rent as soon as we can. We'll ask Mr Burrell . . .'

'He may not be in his office until Tuesday. I guess we'll have to wait till then,' I said unhappily.

'But we can't tell him you think someone is trying to murder us. After all, it may have been an accident.'

'We'll have to tell him, Tim, even if he thinks we're crazy,' I insisted.

'He'll just say it's an old house and the wiring is old-fashioned. Uncle Basil already told him that.'

'Well, OK. We'll ask first about the will, then tell him we want to find a furnished apartment as soon as possible. And maybe I'll tell him about the "accidents" and maybe I won't. But, if we do both die, it would have been better to have let him know . . .'

'Wouldn't help *us* much,' Tim said, more seriously than usual.

'I guess not. But I shan't be happy until we get away from this house, Tim.'

Timothy squeezed my cold hand awkwardly and went away. And I lay awake for a long time, thinking troubled and frightening thoughts. I wanted to live, not to die. I wanted to see Norris again, and to get to know him better, and walk the streets of Manhattan with him as we had walked the streets of London.

CHAPTER 9

The Truth About George

It was after three o'clock before I fell asleep. I just could not abandon the mystery of the exposed wires.

It seemed to me an absolute certainty that someone had deliberately removed the plaster, not only from the wall in front of the wires, but also from where it must have fallen. One flake left in the bath might have drawn the eye to the gap above, and Margaret didn't miss much. I thought it was pretty certain that the job had been done *after* Margaret had been in the bathroom, though.

Grandmother usually took her bath around midday, but, being sick, might not have taken one at all. The danger had been arranged for Tim or me . . . No one could have known which of us would be first to have a bath, but both of us could easily have been involved in a tragedy. For if one had screamed the other would probably have rushed to the rescue. The lock on the bathroom door was broken, and the usual thing was to push an old linen basket in front of the door to keep people out. But it would have been easy enough to get in, and – I shuddered anew at the thought – if someone touched a person being electrocuted then the current reached him, too. I was pretty sure of that.

Grandmother was slightly deaf, and moved slowly, anyway. There hadn't been much chance that she would be the one to go to the rescue. No, the whole thing had been arranged for Tim and me. And there was, after all, the best of reasons for keeping Grandmother alive. If she died the house would be sold, and Uncle Basil and his family, as well as Harry and Nancy, would be homeless.

Anyone in the house could have fixed those wires while Tim and I were out. Uncle Basil was in and out of the main part of the house; so was Aunt Ann. George came less frequently, but his presence would have caused no surprise. He could have been going up to see Grandmother. Harry and Nancy had every right to be anywhere in the house and the job would only have taken a few minutes.

I slept heavily at last and was awakened by Margaret entering with my breakfast tray. Margaret seemed very subdued.

'I keep on thinking you might be dead,' she said.

As soon as I had finished my breakfast I washed and dressed and went to see Grandmother. She was awake and seemed a little better, but she looked terribly frail.

'Nancy told me about the bath, dear,' she said. 'What an awful thing! Basil is going to telephone an electrician as soon as he gets to the office.'

'But I'm quite all right, Grandmother, so please don't worry,' I said.

She gave me a look that was more discerning than usual. 'But you look very pale. It must have upset you.'

It certainly had upset me, and my mind was made up. It was after nine-thirty, so I was going to telephone Mr Burrell's office. I made sure that Nancy was not hovering in the dark passageway, then dialled the number. To my great relief I was told that Mr Burrell would be back by the afternoon, so I made an appointment for three o'clock.

Tim had recovered from his fright and seemed anxious to calm me.

'OK, Mandra, we'll go. But do watch what you say. The main thing is to find an apartment as tactfully as possible.'

'I certainly won't be happy till we're out of here,' I said. 'But, Tim, I'm definitely going home before Christmas. Maybe you could find someone to share the apartment then.'

We took the bus to Chancery Lane, and, as we approached the dark old building, Tim said with satisfaction: 'I feel almost like a Londoner now. If we can find a place of our own I don't see why you want to rush away, Mandra. Except, of course, that Norris Carey . . .'

I blushed. I didn't want to discuss Norris with Tim. 'I like London, too, Tim. I'll come back some day. But I'm sure Uncle Serle doesn't like that new secretary, and I did promise him I'd be back. It will be nice to have money for holidays and clothes, and I want to give Uncle Serle and Aunt Esther some lovely presents, but otherwise I'd like things to go on the way they were before we heard about the Warwick money.'

Tim shrugged in rather an irritated way. I knew he liked the idea of having money, and things wouldn't ever be the way they were, because he could see the world now and all the great art treasures, and work in any country he chose. After this we'd be separated and the thought made me very sad.

Mr Burrell greeted us pleasantly enough, but he made it clear that he was very busy. 'A Birmingham client has died and his affairs are rather complicated,' he explained. 'I may have to go back there tomorrow or the next day. Meanwhile, I can give you thirty minutes. How can I help you?'

Tim glanced at me and I rushed in nervously with my all important question.

'Mr Burrell, what happens to all the money if we die?'

Mr Burrell stared at me, then turned away to fidget with the papers on his desk. 'If you *die*, my dear? You look very young and healthy to me.'

I grew less nervous. It didn't seem a sensible or reassuring answer from a lawyer. 'I'm quite serious, Mr Burrell,' I said, with dignity. 'People die every day. If *I* die, where will the money go?'

'Well, your share of it would go to your brother.'

'And if we both die before we have made wills?'

'You cannot make wills until you are twenty-one. Of course, young people come of age at eighteen now, in Britain, but Mr Warwick was old-fashioned and he fixed the age as twenty-one. The money is tied up until then, except for reasonable amounts for your immediate use. They come from the interest on the capital, you see.'

'But there must be some provision for what happens if we die before we're twenty-one,' I persisted.

'Yes. Well, of course, this was a rather unusual will. Having left nothing to his son Basil or his grandson George, old Mr Warwick then added a codicil to the effect that if you both died before you were twenty-one the bulk of the money should go to Basil Warwick and ten thousand pounds to George.'

'Ten thousand pounds!' I repeated. That was a lot of money, and George had been trying to borrow a mere five hundred pounds. I raised my eyebrows expressively at Tim, who was looking uncomfortable, but startled as well.

'I hardly think you need worry about it,' Mr Burrell said. 'Anyone would be glad to have extra money, but your Uncle Basil doesn't need it. I know almost nothing about his son George, but I suppose the boy is all right. He has a job . . .'

'He sells cars, but doesn't seem very successful,' I told him. I felt awful, for all my worst fears had been realised. George wanted money, and he could have arranged any of the "accidents". Somewhere along the way I had grown used to the dreadful idea of murder, but I knew then that I didn't want it to be George who was so wicked.

'However,' Mr Burrell said briskly, 'you are both alive and well, and I sincerely hope you will stay that way.'

It was my chance and I took it. Tim made a small sound of protest, but I launched myself into the story, as calmly and clearly as I could. I told all the details of the near accidents, aware, as I talked, that Mr Burrell was looking more and more uneasy and unhappy.

'My dear Timandra,' he said, when I had finished, 'you're making very serious, and, I'm sure, totally false accusations. You might even find yourself with an action for slander on your hands. There's a reasonable explanation for each one of those things. Mr Warwick had already mentioned the state of the wiring to me. I really can't allow you . . . It is quite unorthodox. You are not living in a murder story.'

'All the same,' Tim said, with sudden, surprising authority, 'Victoria Lodge is getting on Mandra's nerves. She's never been happy there. So I guess we must find a furnished apartment – a flat – as soon as possible. Can you help us?'

Mr Burrell was still frowning. 'I'm sorry that living at Victoria Lodge hasn't worked out. I had hoped you would manage to adjust to the conditions there. Your grandmother . . .'

'We like Grandmother, but we don't know her very

well,' I said. 'She hasn't given us much chance. And no one could be happy in a place like Victoria Lodge. You've seen it. It's just awful!'

'Old-fashioned, yes, and rather dark, but I should have thought interesting to two young Americans. Still, if you're both quite determined to leave, and in view of the astonishing ideas that have been troubling you, I may be able to find you a furnished flat at least until Christmas. My youngest daughter, Jen, shares one with a friend. It's in a very pleasant district – Chelsea, not far from Sloane Square. I believe that Jen's friend is about to go up to Manchester on a temporary job, and Jen has the chance of working in Paris. Her firm has an office there and they are short-handed at the moment. I know they'd like to sublet for a while. I'll speak to her about it. It would be just the thing, wouldn't it? But how will you tell the Warwick family?'

'Oh, I guess we'll just say we want our own place,' Tim said. 'Nancy's always grumbling about the extra work, you know. And we can still go to see them occasionally.'

'I'll ask Jen to get in touch with you.' Mr Burrell rose, looking relieved that the interview was over. As we walked out of the door he put his hand on my shoulder. 'I quite understand that you're strangers in a strange land, but I advise you to forget what you told me.'

When we were out in the street again I heaved a big sigh. 'Well, I guess you were right, Tim. I shouldn't have told him, but at least we'll get Jen's flat. I feel better when I think of that. But I wish we could leave Victoria Lodge right away. All that money to Uncle Basil and George! And I'm so afraid it's George.'

'Mr Burrell could see an action for slander walking right in at the door,' Tim said. 'He told you to forget it.

But I admit I'll be glad when we're settled somewhere else.'

That evening, after dinner, George walked into our part of the house just as I was coming down the staircase. I jumped at the sight of him and stopped dead, staring down at him. He was smiling and looked more than ever anxious to please.

'Hello there, Cousin Timandra! How about coming to a film?'

'No, thank you, George,' I said.

'Oh, come on! You don't want to spend the rest of the evening in this mausoleum.'

'I'm not staying home,' I said, with relief. 'Tim is taking me to visit an artist friend of his. We're leaving in ten minutes.'

'Well, tomorrow evening, then?'

'I guess not.'

'I thought Americans were supposed to be so friendly.' George sounded ruffled and hurt.

'I don't mean to be unfriendly, George,' I said. 'I have something planned for tomorrow, that's all.' It wasn't true, but I had no intention of going out with him again. How easy it would be for him to push me under a tube train (I had already learned not even to think 'subway') . . .

When I had forgotten George I very much enjoyed the evening.

Tim's friend lived with two others in a big old flat in Soho. On the ground floor of the building was a delicatessen, but we entered by narrow, dark stairs at the side and climbed and climbed. At the very top were three rooms under the roof. The living room was also a studio. Three other girls had been invited and it was like being back in Greenwich Village.

We didn't leave until after midnight and took a taxi back to Victoria Lodge. It would have been just like Nancy and Harry to lock the door, but our keys admitted us and we crept upstairs. I went to bed more cheerfully than I had yet done in London.

The next morning there was a letter from Norris. He wrote warmly, describing his weekend in Liverpool as though he really wanted me to share it with him, but he added the dismaying news that he was afraid he wouldn't be back in London until Thursday. He ended: 'I miss you, Timandra. I think about you plenty, believe me. Best always, Norris.'

So I had to exist somehow until Thursday. I felt keyed-up, alert and suspicious, and I longed to hear from Jen Burrell. More than ever, I hated Nancy's ways and the sharp glances Harry cast at me whenever we met around the house.

That morning Aunt Ann invited me for coffee, but the occasion wasn't a success. She seemed unable to concentrate and looked pale and drawn. She confessed to having a bad headache.

'I'll take some asprin,' she said. 'I haven't been feeling well lately.'

'I thought you seemed kind of worried,' I remarked, trying to be sympathetic, but my words had a startling result. Aunt Ann positively jumped and said very sharply:

'Why should I be worried? I'm busy, that's all. I've a committee meeting at two and another at four. Sometimes I think I'd better give up some of my activities. Worried! What a strange thing to say!'

Well, I'd give her something to worry about. I was curious to see her reaction. 'Tim and I are going to move into a furnished flat,' I announced, and watched her jump again.

'A flat? What on earth for? Surely you're all right here? Your grandmother . . .'

'We can still see her nearly as often as we do now. Mr Burrell agrees. He's finding us an apartment.'

'But I can't see why. Aren't you happy here?'

'No,' I answered bluntly. 'Who could be happy with Nancy and Harry behaving as they do? And the house is so dark and dismal.'

'It isn't very cheerful, I must admit. But . . . Oh, do think about it very seriously before you take such a step. I know George would be upset.'

'George?' I asked, still watching her.

Aunt Ann looked back at me, with an appearance of great candour.

'You don't seem to realise it, Timandra, but George is very much attracted to you. He only said to me last night: "Mother, I don't understand why Timandra is so unfriendly." George is very sensitive, though he tries to seem so worldly and hard. He liked you from the start.'

'We're first cousins,' I said slowly. So had Aunt Ann decided that it would be a good thing for us to marry? Bring the money back into the family?

'Oh, but no one thinks about that these days, if the people concerned are healthy,' she said. So marriage *was* in her mind. Better than murder, anyway.

I said coolly: 'In some states of America they still care. But it doesn't arise. George and I . . .'

'George is a good boy,' Aunt Ann said, putting her hand to her head. 'He'll get on.'

I left her then, feeling very thoughtful. It was better to be married for my money than murdered for it. But if that was the plan then George had no need to try and kill me, at least until he knew it was hopeless.

George knocked on my door that evening just as I was

ready for dinner. 'I never take no for an answer,' he said. 'How about a little outing, Timandra?'

I stared at him and slowly, disconcertingly, he blushed. I came to a sudden decision. I shut the door behind me and gestured toward the staircase.

'Come on down, George. There'll be no one in the living room. Grandmother's gone to bed early.'

'Oh, I say!' George said uneasily. 'You sound awfully stern.'

'It's time we had a talk.' I shut the living room door and went to stand with my back to the fire, facing George. 'Look, George, why do you keep on asking me to go out with you?'

George began to bluster. 'Can't a cousin be friendly? And doesn't it occur to you that I might be . . . well, in love with you?'

'No, it doesn't,' I said forcefully. 'You might as well say you're in love with that table, George. I'd like to be friendly, but we seem to have nothing in common. And I know you have a girlfriend already. And I think you love her.'

George went a kind of puce colour, then turned surprisingly white. He sat down suddenly, and I, suddenly pitying him, sat down also, clasping my hands. I felt I had somehow knifed him; for the first time I had seen genuine emotion on his face.

'How did you know?' George asked, after a moment.

'I saw you with her on Sunday morning. And it looked to me like you were both in love. So . . .'

George groaned, not theatrically, but as if he couldn't help it. 'Yes, it's true. I am in love with Ellie, and she's in love with me. But neither of us has any money, nor any prospect of any, and Mother's been on and on at me, saying what a splendid thing it would be if you and I got married. Keep some of the money in the family and all that. And you don't know how Mother can drive. She's given me no peace since you came.'

'But if you really care about Ellie I don't see how you *can* . . .'

'I'm weak, you see,' George said simply, and I came near to liking him as well as pitying him then. 'Anyone can push me around. Even Ellie says so. I asked Dad to lend me some money, but he wouldn't give me a penny. I make very little money, and Ellie only has a poor kind of job. Not enough for two, and I couldn't live on a woman.'

Not so weak. He sounded genuinely shocked at the idea.

'Then why don't you get a proper job, and make more money?' I suggested. 'Ask your father to give you a job in his firm.'

'Matter of fact, I thought of that.' George leaned forward and spoke earnestly. 'Staying power isn't my strong point, and my brains aren't . . . Well, let's say I've never really tried to concentrate. But, for Ellie's sake, I'd try. Only my father wouldn't even consider the idea. He got really angry and I didn't quite understand why. He kept on saying he couldn't have me in the business. A few years ago he was furious because I wouldn't go in with him.'

'Well, that is kind of strange,' I said slowly.

'Isn't it? All the time until now he's been on and on at me to get a proper job. Then when I say I will . . . But he's been bad-tempered and unapproachable lately. I think something's worrying him. Really worrying him, I mean. Not just that old insult in the will.'

I sat in silence for a few moments, trying to think of a way to help him. Then I had it. 'Why shouldn't you have a job with Warwicks? With Grandfather's firm, I mean,' I said eagerly. 'I'm sure Mr Burrell would fix it if I asked him.'

George leaped to his feet and took my hands.

'Really, Timandra? Would you do that? I would try and work, honestly. Anything to keep Ellie. It's been killing me to think of . . .'

'Marrying me?' I asked gently. I felt very old; almost like George's elder sister.

'Oh, gosh, no! I mean . . . Well, I would have been living on a woman if I'd done what Mother wants. Though of course she says the money you have is Warwick money and we have a right to it.'

I laughed, and after a moment George laughed, too.

'You don't love me. I'm not surprised it nearly killed you to try and go against your love for Ellie,' I said. 'So let's forget all that and just be friends. As for the money, it was unfair we should get it all. It will be better to write Mr Burrell, I think. He's busy right now. He said he might be away. But I'll fix it for you soon as I can, George.'

'I must go and tell Ellie!' George cried. 'But I won't use the telephone here. The walls in this house have ears and I don't want Father to know till it's all settled. He really is behaving strangely at the moment. He never used to be mean, either. He was generous with his money. Well, I'll be off, and thanks a million, Timandra.'

The gong would sound any minute, but I went on sitting there, trying to sort out the conversation that had just taken place. Poor George, I thought. When he became perfectly natural and in earnest he seemed strangely innocent.

Of course, in a way, his love for Ellie gave him a

motive for murder. With Tim and me both dead he would get that ten thousand pounds. But I didn't believe that George would ever have the resolution and wickedness to murder anyone.

So that left us with Uncle Basil, Harry, Nancy or even Aunt Ann. Except that there was no evidence that Aunt Ann had been at Victoria Cottage.

I had definitely eliminated George and I promised myself that he must have his 'proper job'. After that it would be up to him to try and make good.

CHAPTER 10

Overheard In The Fog

I told Tim about George and he was sympathetic, agreeing at once that he must have a job with Warwicks. 'You write Mr Burrell, Mandra,' Tim said. 'And I'll sign the letter as well.'

But I didn't need to do so, for Mr Burrell called the next morning. I was lucky enough to answer the phone, and I was fairly certain there was no one within hearing. Harry had driven off in the old family car, Nancy had gone shopping, and Margaret was cleaning upstairs. Aunt Ann was the only danger, but I could generally hear her steps; she had rather a heavy way of walking.

Mr Burrell greeted me a trifle cautiously. Clearly he had not forgotten our last conversation.

'Well, I have good news for you,' he said, 'and I told Jen I'd let you know myself. They'll be delighted to sublet the flat fairly soon, and Jen wonders if you and your brother would like to go over there this evening to see it. Any time after seven-thirty. I said you'd go.'

'Oh, sure, we'll go!' I said fervently. 'Thank you very much.'

Mr Burrell gave me the address and a few directions for finding the house. Then I took the opportunity to tell him about George. I explained that he wanted to get married and needed a proper job, and that he was keen to work for Warwicks.

'It sounds an excellent idea!' Mr Burrell said heartily.

'There was a time when I hoped that maybe your brother . . .'

'Oh, Tim would never go into business,' I said. 'And George has promised to work hard.'

'But his own father . . . Perhaps I should speak to him first.'

'He won't take George into his own firm. He refused absolutely,' I explained, and hurried on, so that he wouldn't ask questions: 'George is nearly twenty-one. I guess he can take any job offered to him.'

'I'll speak to the manager at Warwicks, then. I'm sure it can be arranged. Well, you and Timothy go and see Jen. I hope you'll find their flat suitable.'

I thanked him warmly and hung up. It looked as if things might work out for us and for George. And I suddenly thought that, when we could handle the money freely, Tim and I could give some of it to our cousin, if he still needed it then. It would be only fair.

I was still in the hall when Uncle Basil startled me by his appearance. Vaguely I had heard footsteps and thought it must be Aunt Ann. He looked very worried indeed.

'I thought you'd gone to the office!' I said.

'No. I've come to explain to Mother. It all happened so quickly, and I thought she'd be upset if Ann said goodbye to her in her present state.'

'Why? What's happened?' I asked, forgetting George,

'Well, Ann . . . She hasn't been herself lately and last night she had a kind of breakdown. Crying and saying she felt ill. So the doctor came first thing this morning and examined her thoroughly. He says there's nothing organically wrong, but she's very low. Hysterical, depressed. He suggests that she goes away for a short while to where she can be well looked after, so I'm just going to drive her out to her mother's. Her mother is a very sensible and energetic woman and a good cook. She's the very one to build Ann up and make her rest. Mrs Clark has a lovely house at Richmond. I'll go and explain to Mother. It's all those wretched committees that have upset Ann.' He disappeared up the gloomy staircase, and I stood fingering the shiny leaves of the plants near the front door.

The news about Aunt Ann didn't surprise me. Something had clearly been worrying her very much, and I was sure it wasn't the committee work. I asked myself if it could possibly be that she knew someone was trying to murder Tim and me. Or was it something else?

Uncle Basil himself had looked simply ghastly. His face had looked puffy and old, though of course no one's face was improved by the light that came through the stained-glass window.

I hated the house more than ever, for the atmosphere of menace and tragedy seemed to be closing in. I must tell Tim about Jen, I told myself, and turned to the staircase. I didn't feel I needed to go and see Aunt Ann. It would only be embarrassing and Uncle Basil hadn't seemed to expect it.

Tim had commandeered a room at the back of the house to use as a studio. The light was better than in most of the rooms and he could have his materials spread around. After some argument with Nancy, who hated the idea, he had succeeded in keeping her out of the place. He had bought an easel and canvasses and was painting as well as drawing. When I entered he was putting the finishing touches to a small painting of Church Walk – a vivid, arresting impression.

He continued to paint as he listened to my story. I could see he wasn't interested.

'You do dramatise everything, Mandra,' he said. 'Aunt Ann is just a bit strained, that's all. A few days at Richmond and she'll be OK again.'

'But something must have upset her, Tim. There are all kinds of strange things going on in this house. Don't you think it's mighty strange that Uncle Basil won't have George in his firm? As if there was something to hide. But Mr Burrell has just been on the phone and he says he thinks it would be a good idea if George worked for Warwicks. And there's one bit of really good news: we're to go and see Jen's flat tonight.'

'OK. Fine. That'll make you feel happier.'

Yes, it will, I thought, as I went to my own room. We just have to get out of this house quickly.

Soon after that I went out to buy some more clothes. I meant to leave London before Christmas, so I thought I might as well buy as many things as possible to take back with me. Woollens were so cheap and good, and then there were the lovely British tweeds. And I had to find presents for Uncle Serle and Aunt Esther. I was looking forward to that.

I spent a profitable and fairly happy day, cheered by the thought that Norris would be back in about twenty-four hours' time.

The warm, sunny days and the foggy evenings had come back again. By the time Tim and I emerged from Sloane Square station and turned into King's Road the mist was thickening. But the shop-fronts in the King's Road were gaily lighted and the pavements were crowded.

'I'm glad we're to be in Chelsea,' Tim remarked. 'Plenty of artists around here, I believe.'

When we left the life and traffic of the King's Road and plunged into dark, quiet streets the mist seemed thicker, but we found the Georgian house where Jen Burrell had her flat without much difficulty.

Jen turned out to be about twenty-five – a pretty, confident girl. She greeted us warmly.

'I was so glad to hear about you,' she said, as she led us into the flat. 'My friend's already gone to Manchester, and I find I can leave for Paris as soon as I'm ready. So I've said I'll go next Wednesday, and you could move in on Thursday morning, if that would suit you? Sit down and be comfortable. Have some coffee first; then you can see everything.'

Tim and Jen did most of the talking, and I sat drinking the very good coffee and telling myself that a week would soon pass. But if only we could have got out of Victoria Lodge sooner!

Apart from the living room, the flat had two bedrooms, as well as a small extra room that the friends used only for storage.

'But it has a good light,' Jen said eagerly. 'You could easily turn it into a little studio, Tim. Look, there's a nice bathroom and the kitchen has everything you'll need. It's expensive and a bit large for us, but we're both in good jobs. We'd only charge you the rent and a little over for the use of our furniture and everything.'

The price she mentioned seemed to me very reasonable, and I could see Tim felt the same. So we agreed and gave her a cheque for the first month. We stayed talking until nine-thirty, when Tim said we'd better go in case the fog was getting bad.

It was, in fact, pretty thick, though better on the King's Road, where there were more lights.

'I like it, in a way,' I said, as we reached Sloane Square tube station. 'It feels like being in a Sherlock Holmes story.'

'Thought you didn't like mystery and murder,' Tim remarked, and I grew sober at once.

'Only in stories. When it seems real, I'm scared,' I confessed.

When we emerged into Kensington High Street the fog was thicker than ever and the traffic was moving very slowly. There were few pedestrians around and I took Tim's arm as we walked up the quiet street that led to Duchess of Bedford's Walk. The big cream houses were almost invisible and even the faint sound of our footsteps was muffled.

'How quiet it is!' I whispered. 'It seems so strange in London. I thought that the first night we came, but now it's quieter than ever. I don't mind it outdoors, though. I always feel safe in London. It's going back to Victoria Lodge that I mind.'

'You could get mugged here just as easily as in New York,' Tim said, ignoring my last remark. 'Well, maybe not quite as easily, but it happens every day. And bombs and shooting. I guess London isn't the safe place I thought it.'

We went on without speaking again until we reached the tiny lane that led to our own gate. The dark laurels hemmed in the driveway and I admitted to myself I was glad Tim was with me. The thought of the brooding house ahead of us made me walk much more slowly. Then my fingers tightened on Tim's arm, for an angry voice had rung out, just around the curve of the driveway.

'I've told you already, Parker, that I haven't got it!' It was Uncle Basil's voice. 'I just can't put my hands on five thousand at the moment. Yes, I know you've been waiting for quite a time; we went into all that. It's no use threatening me, because . . .'

'My dear chap, I wasn't threatening you.' The other voice sounded quiet, urbane, almost shocked. 'It was merely a last reminder that I could do with the cash *and* the interest.'

'You'll get your interest,' Uncle Basil said savagely. 'I've told you, it's only temporary. If you'll wait just a few weeks . . .'

Tim and I had both stopped abruptly. I peered around the bushes and could see the rear-lights of a car glowing through the fog. I guessed that Uncle Basil was standing on the gravel; the other man was probably in the car, as his voice hadn't been so clear.

'Temporary! Well, you may be right. But I've heard rumours that your business isn't very steady – in fact, that it's darned nearly on the rocks.'

'You shouldn't listen to rumours!'

'Well, true or false, Basil? Between friends.'

'Well, false, naturally. There have been a few difficulties owing to a couple of big contracts falling through.'

'Hasn't been all that steady for a while, I heard. I'd hate my money to vanish forever. Shall we say next week?'

'You can say what you like,' said Uncle Basil, with restrained fury. 'Thank you for driving me home. It's unlucky my car had a puncture. Hope you get back all right through the fog.'

The other man made some unintelligible remark, then we heard Uncle Basil's footsteps crunching on the gravel as he walked around to his own front door. The car engine sprang into life.

I drew Tim back into the bushes. 'Don't let him see us!'

The car was turned around and the headlights pierced

the fog. We crouched back into the damp leaves as it went past us. I found that I was shaking a bit and it wasn't with cold, though the damp air was certainly chill.

'Well, I guess we weren't meant to overhear that,' I murmured, as we stepped back on to the driveway.

'We sure weren't,' my brother agreed grimly. 'Maybe we shouldn't have listened.'

'We couldn't help it, with Uncle Basil shouting like that. Anyone could have heard. So he does need money, Tim. He's desperate! No wonder he's looked worried, and Aunt Ann must know all about it.'

'Come on in,' Tim said urgently. 'You're shivering.'

'Not for a minute. He might walk through to our part of the house, and we don't want him to know we were anywhere around. Walk back to the street.'

Tim obeyed me rather reluctantly. 'I don't think you need make too much of it, Mandra. He wouldn't want us to know, but . . .'

'I'll say he wouldn't!' I exclaimed shakily. 'It's a motive for murder, Tim. *Our* murders.'

'Oh, nuts!' But Tim sounded shaken himself. 'Even if he needs the money he wouldn't dare. In the circumstances it would look very suspicious.'

'He might risk that. Well, now we know what was upsetting Aunt Ann. She knew, or guessed, there was trouble. Maybe she only came out with it when she had the breakdown last night, then he had to admit it was true. She'd never stand the shame if he went bankrupt. All those friends of hers on the committees knowing all about it. Tim, I'm beginning to feel sorry for her.'

'Oh, come on indoors, Mandra!' Tim said impatiently. 'You're shaking.'

I allowed him to lead me back to the house and into the usual gloom of the hall.

Nancy was coming down the staircase. 'Coming home in the middle of the night!' she grumbled.

Tim had long since stopped trying to exercise charm on Nancy Cheam, but he answered mildly: 'It's not much after ten-thirty.'

'We're not used to people who keep late hours in this house. What Mr George does is his own business. He uses the other door. I suppose you both want a hot drink? I'll bring you something in the drawing room.'

'Thank you,' I said, ignoring her rudeness. But I couldn't resist adding: 'We won't be bothering you much longer, Nancy. We're moving out on Thursday of next week. We'll tell Grandmother tomorrow.'

Nancy's old, dark eyes flickered over me, but her face showed no expression. 'Going back to America, I suppose. Best place.'

'No. We've rented a flat in Chelsea.'

'I'll get your milk,' the old woman said and disappeared into the dark kitchen passages.

'She only needs a broomstick!' I said bitterly. 'I wish we could leave sooner, Tim. Do be careful. She may put the evil eye on you.'

Tim went into the living room and flung his coat over a chair. Following him, I bumped my arm against the heavy old highboy near the door and winced with pain.

'I've had enough of Victorian furniture!' I cried, and heard the hysterical note in my voice. 'I shan't be happy until we're somewhere else. It may not be the evil eye, Tim, but I can feel some kind of menace closing around us and I'm dead scared.'

CHAPTER 11

Getting Away From Victoria Lodge

The next morning I was awakened by unusual noise out in the passage, and when I opened my door I saw Harry and Margaret standing outside Grandmother's room. Margaret was crying.

The next moment Nancy came out of the room. 'Don't stand there crying, Maggie!' she said harshly. She looked terribly upset. 'Go quickly and ask Mr Basil to come. Tell 'im it's urgent. I think the old lady's gone.'

Margaret fled, looking scared, and I put on my dressing-gown and went out.

Tim was just emerging from his own room. 'What's going on?' he asked.

'It's Grandmother, I guess. Nancy said she thought she was dead. Oh, Tim!'

We went toward Grandmother's bedroom and Harry glared at us fiercely. He was unshaven and he was wearing the large apron he sometimes used when bringing in coal or cleaning shoes.

'I'd keep out of there!' he said.

'But . . .' I didn't feel like taking orders from Harry.

Uncle Basil came running up the staircase. He was dressed for the office, but seemed still to be chewing, as though he had been interrupted while at breakfast. He pushed past Tim and me without seeming to notice us.

'After all, she is our grandmother,' I said and walked softly into the room, which seemed warmer than any other room in the house. Grandmother was lying on the floor near the bed and she certainly *looked* dead. Someone, presumably Nancy, had covered her with a blanket.

Uncle Basil was kneeling down and feeling her wrist. 'What happened, Nancy?' he asked, over his shoulder. 'Did she fall when she got out of bed?'

'I suppose so, Mr Basil. I came in and found her lying there, and her leg looked queer, so I didn't dare try and move 'er. I think the shock must've killed 'er.' Nancy's face was working . . . She looked utterly shaken and grief-stricken.

'Well, she isn't dead,' Uncle Basil told us, standing up again. 'There's a very faint pulse. I'll phone the doctor at once, and I hope to heaven I catch him at home. He'll arrange for an ambulance to come. I wish Ann were here! Even George is away.'

'Has he gone already?' I asked. I had seen George before we went out the previous evening, to tell him about Mr Burrell. He had said he had to go to North Wales on some business to do with the car salesroom, and that they'd said he need not hurry back.

'So I'll probably stay up north until Saturday or Sunday,' George had said. 'I've a friend in Chester. I don't suppose Mr Burrell will be able to arrange an interview for me until next week.'

'He left at seven this morning,' Uncle Basil explained. Then he ran downstairs and Nancy gently raised Grandmother's head and put a pillow under it.

'No need to stand there gaping!' she said fiercely.

Tim and I went to dress, and almost as soon as we were ready the doctor arrived. Five minutes later he was followed by an ambulance and Grandmother was carried downstairs on a stretcher.

The doctor followed and found us hovering unhappily in the hall. 'You're the American grandchildren, aren't you?' he asked. 'Well, I can't say much. She's broken her hip and there's a good deal of shock. She was in no state to stand any kind of accident. Of course she hasn't had much will to live since the old man died, and her heart's not been good for years. But there's always hope, you know.'

Uncle Basil went with Grandmother to the hospital and Tim and I sat down to a half-cold breakfast brought by Margaret.

'Nancy's crying her eyes out in the kitchen,' she told us, still looking rather pink around the eyes herself. 'Oh, I think it's awful! Your grandmother's a nice old soul. I hope she's going to be all right.'

I hadn't cried, but I felt terrible. It seemed so sad. I wished, then, that I had tried harder to get to know Grandmother. The gloomy room, the gloomy old house, seemed worse than ever that morning.

Uncle Basil looked really ghastly when he came back. I almost felt sorry for him, though I was suspicious of him and could never like him.

'I saw her when they'd got her into bed,' he said. 'She was conscious by then and looked fairly comfortable. They gave her a shot and she isn't in much pain. Later, when they think she can stand it, they'll take her into the operating theatre and do something about the hip. I'll have to go to the office now. I told Ann on the telephone and she nearly had hysterics again. *She's* no help.'

'Is there anything *we* can do?' Tim asked.

But Uncle Basil said there was nothing, and he didn't suppose there'd be any news for hours. He didn't intend to try and get in touch with George and ask him to return that evening.

'The fewer people around the better, really,' he said heavily. 'They won't allow any visitors. Just you carry on as usual.'

When he had gone I sighed and said: 'I'm very sorry about Grandmother, Tim, but, if we really can't do anything to help, I'd sure like to get away. Go out somewhere.'

At that very moment the phone rang, and when I ran to answer it it was Norris. At the sound of his voice I felt myself coming alive again. It was such a joyful relief!

'Oh, Norris, are you back?' I cried. 'How glad I am!'

'Something the matter, Timandra?' Norris asked. He was always very quick to sense my different moods. 'Yeah, I'm back in London. I travelled overnight, but the train was delayed by the fog. How about us meeting today?'

'Oh, yes. There's so much to tell you. And it's so awful: Grandmother's had a fall and broken her hip. They've taken her to the hospital. But there's nothing I can do, so I may as well come out. I was just saying to Tim . . .'

'Oh, dear! That's bad.' Norris sounded concerned. 'Well, look. The fog's clearing and it's going to be a fine day. Why don't we take a walk and have a long talk? Then maybe lunch somewhere.'

I arranged to meet Norris at the top of Sloane Street and hung up feeling ten times more cheerful. I felt better still when I was out in the sunshine, though I couldn't forget all the recent events . . . Uncle Basil's angry voice in the fog, Grandmother's old white face as she lay on the stretcher. And I felt a bit guilty about Tim, though he had said he was going to work.

Norris was already waiting and he hugged and kissed me right there on the crowded pavement. I felt warmly happy then, because I didn't think he was normally the kind to be so demonstrative in public. Then he took my hand and we headed into the quiet streets and squares of Belgravia.

As we walked I told him all that had been happening since he went away – about the danger of the electric wires in the bathroom, George and his Ellie, Jen's furnished flat, Aunt Ann's breakdown and the conversation overheard in the fog. I ended with a brief description of Grandmother's accident. It all made quite a tale and Norris listened with grave attention.

'Well, I guess you're both better out of Victoria Lodge as soon as possible,' he said. 'I don't like the sound of those exposed wires, though it is an old house in bad repair. It could have been an accident, Timandra, but it's better to take no more chances. I'm glad to hear about George. Maybe he can he happy. But it's disturbing about your uncle.'

'It gives him a motive for getting rid of us,' I said.

'You know I've been meeting various people my father knows?' Norris remarked. 'Well, one of them works in the City and he told me he knows Basil Warwick slightly. How would it be if I asked him tactfully if he knows anything about his firm? It might be interesting to know for sure if there's danger of bankruptcy.'

'Oh, will you?' I agreed eagerly. 'It's all so worrying, but I think Tim and I had better know. Things seem to be getting worse and worse.'

But I had momentarily forgotten much of the tragedy and trouble by the time we were walking over the crisp fallen leaves in Green Park. Behind us, in the direction of Buckingham Palace, there was stirring music, and London suddenly looked so beautiful in the golden light that I felt a sharp pang of regret at the thought of going away. If only things were different... If only Norris wasn't returning to New York so soon. I wouldn't have wanted to stay without him, even if I had been quite happy at Victoria Lodge. But I supposed I'd have to stay for a few more weeks. Norris was so sane and warm; the one person in the world whose company I really wanted.

Well, if we couldn't stay together in London, maybe we would really meet again in New York, when... when the whole Warwick thing was over. Somehow I had the feeling that there would be a definite end.

I am in love, I told myself, really in love. And, for a time, mystery and danger seemed less important.

During lunch at an expensive little restaurant in Mayfair (Norris always liked to eat in good places) he told me that he would be out of London the next day.

'My father expects me to work, even though it's supposed to be a holiday as well,' he said, a trifle ruefully. 'He keeps on writing to me and sending me introductions to new people. I'm going down to Surrey to see another printing plant, and I've arranged to rent a car for the rest of my time here. I think I can cope with the traffic now.'

'I guess you have to go.' I tried to hide my dismay. Even for one day...

'Sure, I must go, unless it turns out you really need me. If that should happen I'll stay right here in London.' Then, after a moment, he asked: 'Do you really intend to come back home before Christmas?'

'Oh, yes,' I assured him. 'Maybe in the middle of December. Tim would be mad at me if I left any sooner than that. And we'll be OK once we move into Jen's flat.'

He looked at me gravely across the small table. 'It's

good to know that we'll meet again. Let me know the date and flight, and I'll be there to meet you at Kennedy airport.'

'Oh, Norris, will you?' I asked, a little shakily. I didn't want to reveal my whole heart, but the suggestion filled me with joy and relief. Six weeks after he had gone we would be together again. Less than six weeks. I'd pull the date forward as much as I could.

'Sure I will,' he said, smiling. 'I'll count the days. I hate to think of leaving you here, Timandra. I guess I wouldn't be at all easy about it if you hadn't rented that apartment. You and Tim ought to be quite safe there.'

After lunch we walked on through London's sunny streets and crossed to the centre of Trafalgar Square. Norris took a photograph of me surrounded by pigeons and we laughed a good deal. As usual, though, gloom descended on me as I approached Victoria Lodge. I tried to push it away with thoughts of Norris, but even that spell hardly worked as I climbed the Victorian staircase.

Uncle Basil sought out Tim and me before dinner that evening. 'George telephoned from Chester and he's staying there until Sunday,' he told us. 'I said he might as well. Mother stood the operation better than they expected and now she's sleeping. They think she'll probably be all right, but it will be a long business and she must be kept very quiet for a few days. I've permission to slip in when I can, but there can't be any other visitors until Monday or Tuesday.'

'Oh, that's good news!' I cried, with relief.

'I'm just off to have dinner in Richmond now, and I hope Ann's a bit better. But first I want to ask you something. I wondered if you'd like to go to Victoria Cottage for a night or two? You did mention that you'd like to stay there. This house isn't very cheerful for you at the moment, and Nancy is in no state to look after anyone. Even Margaret doesn't seem in her usual spirits.'

Tim and I exchanged glances. I thought he was as eager as I was to get away from Victoria Lodge.

'But ought we to go away when Grandmother's so sick?' Tim asked.

'She won't need you. You can send her some flowers in the morning, with a message, and there's still a telephone at Victoria Cottage. If you were needed I'd let you know, and Harry would drive out and fetch you at once.'

To get away! Oh, how I longed to be some place else. 'Let's go, Tim!' I said.

Uncle Basil went on: 'I thought Margaret could take her weekend off from tomorrow lunchtime. It's due to her, anyway. And Harry'd run you into the country during the afternoon. The house will soon warm up. There are electric heaters and plenty of logs, if you'd like a proper fire. There's even an electric blanket. We persuaded the old man to provide a few comforts there, so there'll be no danger of unaired beds.'

'Oh, we'll manage just fine,' I assured him. 'But won't Harry mind driving us to Victoria Cottage?'

'Harry will do as he's ordered,' Uncle Basil said brusquely. 'And Nancy will see that you have plenty of food to take with you.'

When he had gone I turned to Tim. 'Oh, isn't that just great, Tim?'

'Yeah, I guess so,' Tim agreed. 'It will be kind of fun on our own.'

'But we won't forget danger entirely, Tim. Remember the boat. We'll take very good care that Harry doesn't tamper with the electric blanket.'

Tim looked annoyed at that. 'Oh, Mandra, don't start again, please. We'll be quite safe in the country. We won't use the other boat.'

'I thought,' I said, trying to sound casual, 'that we could ask Norris to join us there on Saturday. He's out of London tomorrow, but he could come Saturday and stay for the weekend.'

'OK. If that's what you want, Mandra.' Tim's eyes met mine, and I knew I was blushing. 'It's serious, isn't it? Between you and Norris?'

'I think so,' I said. 'I mean, I'm dead serious, Tim, but don't say anything to him.'

'In the delicate stage, is it?' My brother laughed.

'I . . . I guess so.' As far as I was concerned I hoped it was for life, but so far there was nothing to tell. Not really, even if I'd wanted to.

The thought of being with Norris in the golden countryside filled me with delight. It would be even better than walking the streets and squares of London. We could stroll by the river, or go up into the hills and walk in the autumn beechwoods. Then we would come back to the house, light an enormous log fire and relax in its warmth. Maybe then the shadows of Victoria Lodge would really recede. With Norris I would feel utterly safe.

CHAPTER 12

Alone By The River

I hated to use the telephone in the hall, because I always felt that someone might be listening. Sometimes it was Nancy, sometimes Harry. More than once I heard the kitchen door shut softly after I had hung up, but several times I had been quick enough to see a quickly retreating back in the gloom of the passage.

Well, it wasn't anything private, of course, but I put on my coat, made certain I had some change, and went out into the gathering fog to the nearest phone-box. I was lucky enough to catch Norris at his hotel. When I explained about going to Victoria Cottage the next day he seemed relieved, and he agreed at once to join us there on Saturday.

'I don't know what time I'll get back to London tomorrow,' he said. 'Maybe late. So I won't try and come then. But Saturday morning will be fine. Oh, yes, sure, I know where it is, Timandra. I looked it up on the map. It will be great to see the house and have a quiet time with you both. Take care until then.'

I returned to Victoria Lodge feeling quite cheerful. Norris would soon have gone home, but the time would soon pass. His promise to meet me at Kennedy was a sure proof that our relationship would not end when he left London.

'Dinner's on the table, Miss!' Nancy greeted me, when I entered the house. She sounded even more unfriendly than usual.

Oh, thank heaven we would be leaving tomorrow! Maybe we could stay in the country until Wednesday, then move into Jen's flat the very next morning. When Nancy had gone I stood for a few moments looking around the hall and up into the gloom of the staircase. The feeling of unfriendliness, even menace, seemed stronger than ever, and I was sure it wasn't all just my imagination.

I had confirmation of this when Margaret came into my room when she was on her way to bed.

'Thank goodness I'll soon be at home!' she cried fervently. 'Nancy has hardly spoken to me all day, and there's something more than usual the matter with Harry. I don't believe it's just the old lady's accident that's upset him, for he cares for no one but himself. All he cares about is feathering his own nest.'

'What do you mean?' I asked. I hated Harry, but I had assumed that he shared Nancy's devotion to the family.

Margaret sat down on my bed and shook back her bright hair. 'He has no heart, if you ask me. He scares me. I think he's hoping to add to that money they were left. I believe he thinks that if he and Nancy stick by the family as long as they're needed, Mr Basil will make it worth their while. After all, the house couldn't run without them, could it? And old Mrs Warwick would be a responsibility.'

I opened my mouth to say that Uncle Basil hadn't any money to give away, but I closed it again. Of course I mustn't say such a thing to Margaret. 'You may be right,' I said instead.

'I think I am,' said Margaret. 'I heard him saying something to Nancy about what they got in the will being a mere flea-bite. He's expecting more from *somewhere*.

Anyway, I'm off at twelve-thirty tomorrow, just as soon as I've finished my work. Oh, it will be lovely to be in a proper normal house. I shall go to a dance in the village on Saturday night.'

'When are you coming back?' I asked.

'Monday morning. I'm going to tell my mother all about it. She won't let me stay when she hears how awful it is.'

That would be just as well, I thought. Victoria Lodge was no place for a girl like Margaret.

'Well, have a nice time,' I said.

When Margaret had gone I lay in the faint red glow from the electric heater and thought about Norris.

The next morning I arranged to have some flowers sent to the hospital, then I did Tim's packing as well as my own. Victoria Cottage would certainly be cold at first, though the morning was sunny, so I made sure we had plenty of warm sweaters. And we had to take our strong shoes for walking, for the country might well be muddy.

I had just finished Tim's packing when he appeared. He said he would take his easel, paints and canvasses, in case it was warm enough to sit outdoors and work. And that would suit me, because it meant that Norris and I could go off alone.

Margaret left at twelve-thirty, and a grim-faced Nancy served lunch for us at one o'clock. It was wonderful to think that we wouldn't have to put up with her rudeness for many more meals. How thankful I'd be to see the last of that gloomy dining room.

We should have left at two o'clock, but Harry came and told us in surly tones that he would have to take the car along to a garage first, as something needed adjusting.

We sat in the hall, anxious to be off; even Tim seemed restless. I went to the phone and called the hospital and was told that the flowers had arrived and been given to Grandmother. She was fairly comfortable and was sleeping a good deal. So maybe we needn't worry. I had a strong desire to forget everything to do with Victoria Lodge just for a few days.

Then, at last, the car returned, and Nancy appeared with two large baskets. 'Here's your stuff,' she said ungraciously. 'You'll find plenty of canned food down at the cottage, and if you want anything more you'll have to go into Henley or walk up to the shop at Hambleden. Mind that basket! It's got two bottles of milk in it.'

In silence Harry loaded the big car and Tim and I climbed into the back. Tim winked at me, as if to say: 'Don't mind Harry's bad temper!' But I did mind, very much. I hated Harry and the atmosphere of dislike and disapproval that emanated from him. I knew that he would listen to every word we spoke, even though he seemed absorbed in coping with the London traffic.

The sun was still shining and the day was remarkably warm for late October. I longed to get the journey over and see the last of Harry. Then we could relax, play our radios very loudly, and settle down to housekeeping. Or camping, if it turned out to be more like that.

'I'm going to ask Mr Burrell if I can have enough money to buy a small car,' Tim said presently, in a low voice. 'There are some very nice little British ones. Don't you think that would be a good idea, Mandra?'

'Yes, I do,' I whispered back. 'When you go back to New York you can either sell it or have it shipped over.'

Tim looked at me sideways, a little embarrassed. 'Maybe I won't be going back, Mandra. Not for about a year, anyway.'

'A year?' I forgot to keep my voice down, and I saw Harry's ears twitch.

'You knew I might study art in Europe,' Tim murmured.

'But a *year* . . . it seems so long.' Yet I didn't mind as much as I would have done even quite recently. Somewhere along the way I must have accepted that I had really lost my twin. It had been bound to happen, of course, as we became adults. One or both of us would marry . . . marry! I thought of Norris, and tried to imagine him walking around the printing works. He had not said in so many words that he loved me, but he had said that he would count the days until he met me at Kennedy. That was comfort and joy enough. And I would see him the next morning.

Harry didn't speak a word all the way. He drove fast once the worst of the traffic was left behind, and he certainly drove well. His thin, worn hands were steady and confident on the wheel, and he looked as if he really enjoyed handling the big car – if Harry could ever be said to enjoy anything.

We did not go the way George had taken us. By the time we passed through Medmenham, a village close to the Thames, the sun had gone in and the sky was grey, but the hills that rose on our right still looked beautiful. The beechwoods had flamed into their full autumn glory, russet and gold and red. I had seen the autumn colours in New England, and maybe they were finer, but the Chiltern Hills of England came a very close second. More fields had been ploughed and the grey-white earth surged up to the edge of the triumphant woods.

Harry spoke at last, as he stopped the car outside Victoria Cottage. 'I'll just come in and see that everything is in working order,' he said.

'Oh, please don't bother,' I answered quickly, for I didn't want Harry in the house.

But he ignored me and began to take our possessions out of the boot. Then he went straight to the front door and opened it with his own key. We had keys, too, given to us by Uncle Basil.

I stood on the gravel, stretching and breathing deeply. 'How still it is, Tim,' I said. 'And quite warm, though the sun has gone in. What lovely smells!'

Some roses were still blooming, but fallen petals lay all over the beds. I thought that tomorrow, before Norris came, I would do some gardening. I knew almost nothing about it, but anyone could pick up rose petals and cut off dead heads.

We carried in the baskets and Tim's painting things, and heard Harry moving around in the kitchen regions. We both went upstairs and Tim said he'd have George's room, while I chose a little one that had a window looking toward the river. The water was shining in the grey light and the overgrown lawn looked very green.

'I'm going down to see what Harry is up to,' I said, and Tim groaned.

'Why, Mandra? Do relax. What can he be up to?'

'I don't know, but remember the boats,' I said, and went softly back down the stairs. My feet made no sound as I crept along the passages and I peered cautiously into the kitchen. Harry seemed to be occupied harmlessly enough. He had just set the refrigerator going and was turning to deal with the fire. There was coal in a big box and logs and kindling in another, and I heard him whistling between his teeth as he worked.

When the fire sprang into life he fetched a bucket and

put coal and kindling into it, and I guessed that he was going to start the living room fire. So I slipped quietly away and carried my suitcase upstairs.

Harry followed me five minutes later and found me unpacking. 'I'll show you where the blankets and sheets are kept, Miss,' he said. 'And you can use the electric blanket to air the beds. I've lit the fire in the kitchen and another in the sitting room, but if you don't want to bother there's a heater in there you can use tomorrow.'

'Thank you, Harry,' I said awkwardly, following him to cupboards in the passage. I only wanted to get rid of him.

'And if you want hot water there's an immersion heater in the bathroom. Come and I'll show you. Know when you want to go back to London?'

'Well, no. I guess we don't,' I said quickly. 'We'll call when we decide. Unless, of course, Grandmother is worse.'

'Well, just telephone when you want to be fetched. Is there anything else?' I'd never before heard him make such long speeches, and I shook my head. 'Then I'll get away now. As it is I'll run into the rush hour traffic.'

'I'm sure he'll miss it, actually,' I whispered to Tim, who had emerged from his room and been listening. 'It's nearly quarter-to-five now.' Harry had stumped downstairs.

'Well, let's do the beds,' Tim said cheerfully. 'Then we can switch on the electric blanket and the first one should be aired in an hour.'

We carried sheets, pillowcases and blankets and set to work, but after a few minutes I raised my head and listened. I couldn't hear a sound below.

'Has Harry gone, Tim? I didn't hear the car leave.'

Just at that moment I heard a faint click: the shutting

of the front door? Tim went to his window, which was over the front porch.

'He's getting into the car right now. There he goes!'

'Well, I sure am glad,' I said. 'But what's he been doing? I don't trust him, Tim. Take care he hasn't tied string across the staircase or something like that. He had time enough.'

Tim looked annoyed, as I had known he would. 'Mandra! Why should he?'

'So we'll break our necks,' I said. 'Well, we'll be careful, and now we're free and alone. But isn't it going dark and misty? He'll run into fog, and won't he be mad?'

'It's going to rain,' Tim remarked.

'Well, never mind. We'll draw the curtains presently and be really homey. The house is cold, but it will get warmer.' We had electric heaters on in both bedrooms.

'Central heating would be a fine idea,' said Tim.

'Yes it would,' I agreed. 'Maybe we'll have it put in one day. But I'm growing used to being cold indoors. I'm hungry, Tim.'

'So am I, but we can't have a meal until everything's done.'

By the time we had made both beds, found towels and done what unpacking seemed necessary, the mist was pressing against the windows and it was raining. Though it was still not really dark we turned on lights all over the house.

The little living room was growing quite warm, but I put more coal on the fire.

'I hope it isn't going to keep on raining,' I said. 'I want to go walking with Norris in those wonderful woods on the hills. I like this room, don't you? The window looks toward the river and we could open the French doors if the sun were shining.'

'It's just pouring with rain now,' said Tim, peering into the misty gloom.

'Well, pull the curtains across and let's be cosy. I'll put a log on top of the coal. Wood fires are kind of nice. What a relief it is to be alone, and no Harry or Nancy to glare at us. I feel we may be safe here, Tim, now Harry's gone. Though I hope he hasn't left some kind of booby-trap.'

'Of course we're safe,' Tim said impatiently. 'We won't go on the river in this weather.'

When we went along the passage to the kitchen the fire had burned up brightly. Tim began to unpack the baskets of food, while I peered into the cupboards.

'There's enough food to feed us for a month,' I said. 'If we don't mind sticking to cans. Is there any coffee? There's none here.'

'Yes,' said Tim. 'Nancy's packed coffee and tea, and sugar, butter, eggs and bacon. Oh, and half a cold chicken and some salad. Shall we have the chicken and salad now?'

'Bread?' I asked.

'Two loaves. Nancy may hate us, but she didn't mean us to starve.'

'Well, you carry the things in,' I ordered. 'Don't forget cups and plates and knives and forks. I'll make the coffee. I suppose the percolator works?' And I examined it cautiously, remembering those electric wires. But it seemed all right. 'I'll have mine black. I like it and it will save the milk. We don't know where we can get any more.'

But Tim was eyeing the bottles eagerly. 'We'll find somewhere tomorrow. I'm mighty thirsty. Mind if I have some milk now?'

'OK. But it'll be warm. Put the other bottle in the refrigerator. The coffee won't be long.'

Tim found a glass and poured himself some milk. He drank it quickly. 'That's better!' he said, and began to pile things on a large tray.

I waited for the coffee to be ready, with my little radio playing. The kitchen looked cheerful and I felt very happy. I thought with amazement that, less than one month earlier, I could not have imagined Tim and me alone in an old flint house by the River Thames in England.

Life was very strange, very unexpected. In so few weeks we had been left a lot of money, had grown familiar with London and I, at least, had learned to face the idea of danger and death. But both seemed remote at that moment. I had met Norris, and that was the most important thing of all. Without Norris life would feel quite different. Being in love diminished everything else.

The coffee was ready. I found a coffee-pot, but there did not seem to be a milk jug, so I decided that the opened bottle would do to carry into the living room.

Tim had arranged two small tables by the fire and put out chicken and salad. We'd forgotten bread and butter, so I ran back to the kitchen and put one of the loaves on an old wooden bread board.

'Here's the knife,' I said. 'Just cut what you want and a piece for me. I'll pour the coffee. Want milk in it?'

'Oh, sure.'

'It's a pity there's no cream,' I said. 'Maybe we can get some tomorrow. There were farms in the Hambleden Valley; I remember when we came with George. Surely English farms sell milk and cream? I suppose Nancy never thought of it. She doesn't understand the way we like our coffee. I hate it the British way with hot milk.'

We settled down contentedly to eat and drink. It was wonderful to be quite on our own with the world shut out.

'Listen to the rain!' said Tim. 'Harry won't have much of a drive back to London.'

'Let me tell you something,' I said gaily. 'I don't really care if he drives into a flood.'

The sound of the sluicing rain somehow added to my pleasure. It made the warm, shabby old room more attractive and more our special refuge. Of course the woods would be terribly muddy tomorrow and maybe the downpour would bring off some of the gorgeously red and gold leaves. But the country always smelled delicious after rain and Norris surely wouldn't mind a bit of mud.

'It's like coming out of a nightmare,' I said presently. 'The nightmare of Victoria Lodge and that awful staircase going up into the gloom. And people watching and listening – all the tensions.'

And I did not know then that the nightmare was, in fact, very near at hand.

CHAPTER 13

Timandra's Nightmare

Tim had drunk a third cup of coffee and was lying back in his chair. I was talking eagerly about Jen's flat and at first didn't notice that he was not replying. Then I looked across at him in surprise.

'Tim!' I cried. 'What's the matter? Are you sick?'

'No,' he answered, in a blurred voice. 'Not sick. Just . . . just kind of sleepy.'

'But you're never sleepy in the daytime, Tim.'

'Am now,' Tim told me, and gave a huge yawn. 'You play your . . . your radio. Just let me sleep.'

I looked at him with exasperation. He wasn't being a very lively companion. But I reached for my little radio and tuned it in to some music.

I sat peacefully enough for fifteen minutes, too comfortable to start clearing away our meal or to find one of the books I had brought with me. Actually, there were plenty of books in a bookcase against the far wall. Maybe there was something interesting there, if only I could be bothered to get up. I wasn't at all sleepy, it was just that it was so pleasant.

Then suddenly I sat upright and stared at Tim. He seemed to be breathing far too heavily, and his face was very flushed.

'*Tim!*' I shouted, leaping to my feet and sending a plate crashing off the table. I had gone suddenly very cold and a sharp fear shot through me.

My loud voice and the crash did not disturb Tim. He didn't move or open his eyes, but his breathing seemed to go louder. I could hear it even over the soft music. I turned off the radio and bent over Tim, shaking him violently. His head lolled.

I knew then, with mounting fear, that he had been drugged. But how? Why? I looked wildly around and my gaze lighted on the milk bottle, almost three-quarters empty. Milk was the only thing Tim had had that I had not shared.

I seized the bottle and sniffed at it, but it only smelt of milk. I thought back to the time in the kitchen, to when the bottles had been on the table. The usual metal caps had been on both bottles. I could remember Tim raising one with his finger-nail.

Thoughts whirled through my mind. So someone had put something in the milk, then had fixed the metal caps on again, and Tim had drunk my share as well as his own. If I had had milk, too, I would be in the same drugged sleep. And anyone at Victoria Lodge could have known that we were great milk drinkers. Nancy had several times grumbled about the higher milk bills; as if it had anything to do with her how much we drank! But even Uncle Basil and George could have known. But George (and his mother, of course) had been away, and Nancy had packed the baskets. Nancy!

Nancy, the old witch, who hated us and sometimes seemed not quite right in the head. But Tim didn't look poisoned; he looked, and sounded, as if he had had an overdose of sleeping pills.

People could die from an overdose, and no one would have found us in time to do anything. Probably not even Norris would have arrived in time in the morning. Of course no one knew that I had invited Norris to join us at

Victoria Cottage. I was sure it had not been mentioned in anyone's hearing.

But if we had been found dead there would have been an investigation. It would have been a clear case of murder.

All these thoughts probably took only a few seconds, then I realised that I must do something about Tim at once. Wake him up somehow, then keep him awake.

I slapped his face hard, shouting so loudly that the sound echoed frighteningly around the room. It had no effect at all. I tried to pull him upright, but, in spite of his slim build, he was too heavy for me and he simply slipped back into the chair, his legs sprawling.

'Tim! Oh, Tim! Wake up!'

Black coffee: that was what you gave people, I remembered, with a gasp of relief. I peered into the coffee pot and saw that there was a little left. It was probably cold, but I poured some into a cup and tried to force it into Tim's mouth. But the coffee merely ran down his chin and on to his sweater.

It was no good. I needed help and I must have it quickly. Cold, shaking, but with a fairly clear head, I rushed into the hall and seized the phone book. There must be some doctors listed. But it was not a classified directory and I gave it up after a moment. In England you dialled 999 if there was a fire, or you wanted the police or an ambulance. That way I'd get help quickly.

But the phone was dead. I dialled over and over, desperately, but I knew it was no use. I would not get help that way. It must be out of order. Maybe the heavy rain, or . . . I remembered that Harry had not driven away immediately. I had not been able to find that he had done anything, but the answer seemed plain now. A moment's search in a dark cupboard proved to me that the wires had been cut.

There must be a reason. Harry was not out of his mind. If he had cut the wires (and who else?) there was some definite, diabolical plan.

I ran to the kitchen, soaked a cloth in cold water and returned to the living room. Tim had slipped down still further and was breathing very stertorously. Again and again I flicked the cloth across his face, shouting loudly. Tim stirred and for a moment I felt hopeful, but it was no good. He wasn't going to be roused that easily.

I glanced at my watch and saw that it was nearly seven o'clock. I went to the window and drew back one of the curtains, peering out into mist and complete darkness and into rain that was pouring down the panes. Where was the nearest house, the nearest phone? I asked myself. There was no other house down our own lane, but there were some on the main road: cottages . . . other buildings at Mill End . . . maybe even a phone-box, I couldn't remember. At any rate there would be passing cars, but would any of them stop on such an awful night? I'd have to try, though I shrank from the thought of braving the downpour and the intense country darkness. It was then that I realised I'd forgotten to bring a flashlight.

I went upstairs for my raincoat, which I'd put into the wardrobe. It had been designed for city wear and wasn't going to be much protection against such rain. But there were some old umbrellas in the hall and I took one. It didn't really matter if I got wet, so long as I was able to get help for Tim.

The house all around me was deadly silent, except for the distant, steady hiss of the rain. I took a last look at Tim, then opened the front door and stared out into the mist and the intense blackness. There wasn't even an outside light over the porch to guide me a little, help me to see the curve of the driveway.

I left the door open, but the light from the hall was swallowed up in the mist before I had gone three yards. I set off gropingly, heading toward where the driveway should be, and stumbled on to a rose bed. The sharp thorns tore my hands and I cried out with pain. I turned around and thought I could see the dim light where the house was. So I must aim away from the light, keep over to the right, then veer left.

I fell headlong. The umbrella shot away from me and a sharp pain went through my left ankle. I had tripped over one of the big rocks that edged the gravel. For a few moments I lay on the wet grass of the border, too much winded and in pain to think clearly.

When I tried to rise the pain in my ankle was so agonising that I knew I'd never walk upright. There wasn't the faintest hope of my getting to the gates, let alone the main road. The most I'd do would be to crawl back to the house.

I wasn't really sure, at first, if I was going in the right direction. The dim light might be an illusion. There were deep pools on the gravel and the rain fell into my eyes.

But I reached the front door and hauled myself upright with the help of the trellis that held the climbing roses. Back in the hall, with the door shut, I sat on an old wooden chair until I felt less sick and faint. My trousers were soaking wet and the rest of me, including my hair, wasn't much better. I'd started off with a scarf tied over my head, but that had gone. My dirty hands were grazed and painful, and blood was mingling with the earth and gravel.

When at last I tried to stand on my injured foot I managed it, though the pain was savage. I tried again and found I could bear it. It was probably just a bad sprain, and might get easier in time. Meanwhile, what about Tim?

I flung aside my raincoat and hopped into the little cloakroom off the hall to wash my hands. When I saw my white face in the mirror, with the clinging tendrils of wet hair, I hardly recognised my own reflection. I was half-crying and I hadn't even known it. I looked like a ghost.

Somehow I reached the living room. Tim had not moved and the broken plate still lay on the floor. I could hardly believe that the scene was real. It must be some nightmare from which I would soon wake. But the pain in my ankle and hands seemed real enough.

I sat down and cried then, in earnest. There was no one to see my weakness. Maybe the pain in my ankle would lessen a bit and in thirty minutes or so I'd try again to fetch help. If I did nothing Tim might die.

Maybe I fainted. I know I closed my eyes and sank back in the chair. Then I was aware again, for I had heard a sound outside. Could it have been a car stopping? I jumped up, was stabbed by the pain in my ankle, and dropped down again. I tried again more cautiously and began to move toward the door, clutching on to the furniture. And then, with the door half-open, my hand on the kob, I stopped. Instinct told me that it was no rescuer . . . It must be an enemy.

I had not remembered to lock the front door and it was opening softly. I heard it close, then footsteps on the polished floor of the hall. I let go of the doorknob and pressed myself against the wall. It was the worst moment of that terrible evening.

It was Harry who entered the room. Harry, wearing his old overcoat and with rain shining on his thin grey hair. For a moment he stood just within the room, staring at Tim. Then his glance moved around and he saw me, pressed against the wall near the door, rigid with fear.

He looked, for a fleeting second, extremely taken aback. Dimly I realised that he had expected to find us both asleep and helpless.

We exchanged looks for what seemed a long time, then I gasped: 'What do you want, Harry? What have you done to my brother?'

Harry kicked the door closed, then slowly took off his coat, putting it neatly on the nearest chair. When he turned around he had a gun in his hand. I stared at the weapon without at first believing in its reality. In spite of the violence in New York City, I had never before in my life seen anyone handling a gun.

I had not moved from the wall behind the door. Harry waved the gun at me and said in his harsh Cockney voice: 'Come on now. Go and sit in that chair near your brother.'

I started to obey, limping badly, and he stared at me suspiciously.

'No tricks, mind. This gun's loaded. Why are you walking like that?'

'I fell and sprained my ankle,' I told him. 'I was going for help for Tim. I fell. Look at my hands and my trousers are soaking wet.

He gave a harsh laugh as he looked at the hands I held out to him. 'Was that why there was an open umbrella on the drive? Gave me the fright of my life! Wondered what it was, at first. You'll have worse than injured hands, my girl. Now remember: one move and I'll shoot.' He had seen my eyes light on the bread knife that still lay on the board beside the loaf. He picked it up and flung it into a corner, and I saw he was not going to give me the slightest chance to attack him, or escape. And how could I really do either, with an injured foot and bleeding hands? Still, his eyes never left me.

'You wouldn't dare to shoot,' I said, with the boldness of desperation. 'How would you explain the – the body?'

'Never you mind. Now you sit down and keep still. I want to look at your brother.' He bent over Tim, and slapped and shook him, but there was no response. 'Well, this one's out all right. Pity you didn't drink some milk as well. It'd have been pleasanter for you. As it is . . .'

I crouched in the big chair, watching Harry. He looked small, old and ordinary, yet terrifyingly determined. He didn't look in the least mad, unless his inhuman disregard for my fear could be called madness. He looked like a man who had a job to do, and who meant to get it done quickly.

'I don't know why you came back,' I said. I wanted to get him talking, wanted to deflect his purpose, whatever it was. Though I had really no hope at all that help would come.

Harry moved to the fire and stood with his back to it, weighing the little gun in his hand. 'The plan was that I should leave it as late as possible, but it's such a rotten night that I couldn't drive around any longer. Seemed no point in it. I thought you'd both be sleeping like birds in their nests.' He chuckled at the picture, then frowned. 'Birds in their nests: good, i'n' it? There's one bird that won't feel the water. He'll sink like a stone and the current'll carry him well away from here. With luck, he might not be found for days.'

'In the *river*?'

'In the river,' Harry repeated mockingly. 'In dear old Father Thames. What you might call a watery grave. And you as well, my girl. Because you're going to drink some milk, too.'

I glanced involuntarily at the milk bottle and Harry

laughed. 'More in the kitchen, no doubt. Nancy gave you two bottles and both were well treated.'

'Nancy put the stuff in?' I asked shakily.

'Not 'er. Nance knows nuffin' about it. Not that it'll help the old girl much if anything goes wrong. There'll only be her finger-prints on the bottles, and yours, of course, and the milkman's. I put the stuff in and I wore gloves. I read detective stories, see.'

'But . . . why?' I asked, in a daze of horror.

'Oh, don't give me that! You're not a stupid girl. To get you and that brother of yours out of the way, o' course. Then the money'll go where it ought to go. All that lovely lolly!'

'But what would *you* get out of it? And what has Nancy done that you want her to . . . to take the blame?' My mind was starting to work, but my main idea was still to keep him talking.

Harry laughed harshly. 'Got to have a scapegoat, haven't we? And Nance'll do as well as anyone. She's given me an awful life. You wouldn't know about anything nasty like that. You're a privileged girl. Makes it all the more satisfying to do you in. I never had a chance, see. Grew up in an orphanage – not one of them lovely, kind places, but a lousy dump, where we were beaten and kicked around. Weren't the same, fifty, sixty years ago. Not always, anyway. Then I left and got a lousy job and I never had no money to speak of, and worst of all I married Nance. Or she married *me*. Ten years older, and a stronger character, and she was determined to get me. She was working for the Warwicks, o' course, and I went there, too. Well, it's going to be different now. I'm going to live me own life . . . maybe a trip to Spain or some other place where the sun shines.'

I had listened with something that was like dawning

pity. It was a sad and dreadful story. There was always a reason, perhaps, for wickedness. That little boy in the orphanage, hating everyone, had led directly to the old man who faced me then, bitter and triumphant.

'But . . .' I began.

'It was broadly hinted to me,' Harry went on, 'that I would get ten thousand quid if you two kicked the bucket. Know what that means, don't you, even if you are American? I had a few other little tries, just getting me hand in, as you might say. This time it's going to be dead easy, even with you still bright-eyed and alive.'

'You must be *mad*!' I cried, forgetting pity. Terror and despair washed over me. Norris . . . Uncle Serle and Aunt Esther . . . They would never know what had really happened. Oh, I would never return to New York and be met by Norris at Kennedy.

'I'm sane enough,' Harry told me casually. 'It's foolproof. Your bodies will be found sooner or later in old Father Thames and it will pretty certainly be assumed that one of you fell in and the other went to the rescue. With luck there'll be no autopsy, but, if there is, and they find some of your Grandma's sleeping stuff, then there'll be the two milk bottles here to prove where it came from. And then they'll think you went in when you were dazed, and poor old Nance will take the rap. Hates you, doesn't she? And not quite right in the head. And I shall have the ten thousand pounds and be rid of the old woman.'

'Let me tell you something,' I said, in a shaking voice. 'You may not be mad, and I see you had an awful life, but you sure are the wickedest . . .'

'Well, blame your grandfather. That's where the trouble started.'

'You mean the will?' I whispered. 'Not leaving Uncle Basil anything? It *must* be Uncle Basil . . .'

'Of course it was your Uncle Basil, dear. Now shut up and let's get moving. That brother of yours is out for quite a time, by the look of him. But I'm not taking any more chances. Mr Basil needs the money, and it's only fair he should have it, with a nice slice for yours truly. Pour that milk into a cup and drink it. Then we'll get the other bottle.'

I stared at him and he stirred impatiently.

'Go on. Pour it into a cup. Don't tell me you want a clean one?'

My hand was cold and shaking, but I reached for the bottle. I had the wild idea of throwing it in Harry's face, but then his finger would press the trigger. I was convinced by then that he would stop at nothing. He wouldn't even be deterred by the risk of a body with a bullet in it. That he couldn't blame on Nancy.

I poured the remainder of the milk into a cup and Harry looked gloomily at the small amount. 'I think,' he said, 'that we'll take a little walk into the kitchen now.'

'I – I can't walk that far. My ankle . . .'

'Oh, it'll carry you that far. Come on!' Harry began to move toward the door, walking backward and never taking his eyes off me. 'No tricks, mind.'

I rose slowly. My ankle stabbed me with pain, but held firm. I began to walk toward Harry, clutching on to the back of a chair. I knew it was the end. I had the strange, mesmerised feeling that Harry could make me drink the milk, and once I had done that the results were certain.

The rain was still pouring down outside and the wind seemed to be rising. The living room door, which Harry had not kicked quite shut, was beginning to open. Harry, with his back to it, was unaware of the fact.

And then, incredibly, Norris was there, dripping wet

and holding a heavy walking stick. He brought it down hard on Harry's right shoulder. Harry gave a startled grunt of pain and dropped the gun harmlessly on the carpet.

'Pick up the gun, Timandra,' Norris ordered calmly. 'Keep him covered.'

I obeyed.

CHAPTER 14

The End Of Danger

The blow had been a heavy one and it had bewildered and probably half-stunned Harry. Norris began to propel him toward a chair and Harry collapsed into it.

'Broken me collar bone, I wouldn't wonder,' he muttered thickly. His left hand caressed his right shoulder.

'Oh, *Norris!*' I cried. I was shivering violently with reaction. 'How did you get here? I thought . . .'

Norris took the gun from me, examined it briefly, then held it expertly. He was pale and his hair was wet. I could hardly believe in his reality.

'Hardly time for explanations,' he said. 'But I returned to London earlier than I expected. I tried to call you here at about five, but there was no reply and I was told the line seemed to be out of order. So I decided to drive straight out here and not wait for the morning. I drove pretty fast, in spite of the mist and heavy rain, but I had a little difficulty in finding this place. I left my car in the lane and walked the last bit. I had a feeling there was trouble and that I'd better not advertise my presence. The other car was outside and the front door was ajar. I just walked in, and then I heard Harry's voice and listened. The only weapons around were some old umbrellas and this stick. Seems to have done the job well enough.'

Harry glared. 'I'll have the law on you. Might have killed me.'

Norris waved the gun thoughtfully. 'I guess not. You're not in a position to go to the police after what I overheard. Your collar-bone isn't broken. You can move your arm OK.'

'There's no evidence,' Harry said quickly. 'Only that the sleeping stuff was in the milk and Nancy will be blamed for that. I'll just say I turned back 'cos of the bad weather and meant to spend the night here. And if the boy dies . . .'

Norris glanced at Tim and his expression was troubled. But he said quietly: 'There *is* evidence.' He put his hand into his pocket and partly revealed a small object. 'A pocket tape recorder. My latest toy. I little thought, when I bought it, that I'd record such an illuminating conversation. Yeah, Harry, there's enough evidence to get you ten years in prison. And, of course, if Timothy dies, it will be murder.'

Harry gave a choked cry and started to rise, but Norris waved him down again.

'What are we going to do, Norris?' I asked. My brain was growing clearer. 'We – we have to do something about Tim at once.'

'Sure we must,' Norris agreed. 'But first we'll tie Harry up. Can you go and find some rope? Or very strong string?'

I started to obey, forgetting my injured ankle. I staggered and nearly fell and Norris involuntarily turned to help me. And in that moment Harry acted. The table near him went over, he seized the coffee-pot in his left hand and hurled it at the gun. The gun fell to the floor for the second time and Harry pushed me toward Norris so violently that we clung together, swaying.

A second later Harry was out of the room, slamming

the door. By the time we had recovered the front door had slammed also.

'Oh, we must stop him!' I shouted.

Norris bent down and grabbed the gun, but by the time he reached the front door the car had already driven away into the rain.

He came back, smiling ruefully. 'May as well let him go. I'm not much of a shot, especially in rain and mist.'

'Maybe your car's blocking the lane . . .?' I suggested, but he shook his head.

'I guess not. He'll get past. Never mind, Timandra. We've had quite a lot of luck already tonight. That gun might have gone off when I hit Harry. I knew I was taking an awful chance. And again when he threw the coffee-pot. We're alive, and Harry won't bother us again.'

'And we have the evidence,' I said. 'Your tape recorder . . .'

Norris drew me back into the living room. I had managed to get as far as the doorway.

'I'm afraid that was just spur of the moment cleverness,' he said. 'But maybe it will have the desired effect. If they both believe that there is evidence . . .'

'But you showed it to him!'

'Just something I had in my pocket.' Norris displayed the little box. 'You do get tape recorders around this size and he seemed to believe me. Now, come on, Timandra. We have to get working on your brother. Can you walk well enough to help, my dear love?'

I made a valiant effort, helped by those last three words. 'I'm OK. But I did everything I could think of, Norris, before Harry came. Slapped him with a wet cloth, and shouted, and tried to give him black coffee.'

I stood looking down at Tim. He was still very flushed and breathing heavily.

'It needs two, though you did all the right things. I suppose we can't call a doctor? The phone . . .?'

'I tried to do that, but Harry cut the wires when he bought us here. We could put Tim in your car.'

'And get lost in the mist. Besides, if we can bring him round ourselves it will save explanations. Unless you want to bring this whole thing to court? Attempted murder . . .'

'I don't know,' I said. 'I guess Harry's right, and the only evidence is against Nancy. She's been just awful, but I'd hate to have her blamed.'

'Right. Let's get on with it.'

Norris took off his coat and told me to go and make the strongest coffee possible.

'I think he's improving,' he said suddenly. 'Isn't his breathing better? And that high colour is fading.'

It was true, I saw in wild relief. In the last minute or two there had been a change. I left Norris working on Tim and went slowly into the kitchen, leaning on the walking stick that had saved us all. When the coffee was ready I went back to say I didn't think I could carry it safely, and Tim's eyelids were fluttering. Very soon he was sitting up, looking dazed. He managed to drink a good deal of the coffee, but still showed signs of wanting to sleep again.

'Leave me alone!' he said. 'Just let me . . .'

'I'll walk him around,' Norris said, and, in spite of Tim's protests, he kept him moving around the house for twenty minutes. Then we gave him some more black coffee and full awareness gradually returned to Tim's face.

'He's going to be all right!' I cried.

'Of course I'm all right,' Tim said crossly. 'What's all the fuss about? I don't understand what happened.'

Norris explained briefly and Tim looked astonished and indignant.

'Mean to say I just lay there while all that was going on?'

'You're lucky not to be lying in the river,' Norris said grimly. 'Timandra, you go to bed and sleep. Tim and I will stay up all night. I don't think he should sleep again just yet. In the morning we'll decide what to do.'

He had been gently urging me into the hall as he spoke. I got as far as the foot of the stairs, then turned around to look at him doubtfully. I felt worn out and rather desolate suddenly.

Tim was still in the living room and the door was nearly closed. Norris put his arm around me and held me closely.

'Tim's OK, I promise. I'll look after him. I don't believe he had so very much of that sleeping stuff. Not a lethal dose. Harry only wanted you to have enough of the stuff to sleep soundly.'

'Then he'd have dropped us in the river,' I whispered, starting to tremble. 'But Tim had my milk, too, Norris.'

'Even so, he's all right now. Go to bed and remember that I love you. When I heard Harry threatening you . . . Well, I really knew long before that.' He kissed me and pushed me gently up the stairs.

'Good night, honey. I'll lock all the doors and windows, but nothing more will happen tonight.'

I gave Norris a last look, then went to my room. I undressed and almost fell into bed. The bed was very cold, because we had never had a chance to change over the electric blanket. Tim's would be lovely and warm and he wasn't going to use it. But, even as I thought this, I was drifting into sleep, lulled by the steady falling of the rain.

The rain had stopped, and the mist was clearing, as we packed up our things after breakfast and prepared to leave Victoria Cottage. Tim looked rather pale and drawn, but otherwise he seemed to have suffered no ill effects. He was in fairly good spirits and had eaten some breakfast.

We had decided that Tim and I would take rooms at Norris's hotel before we did anything about Victoria Lodge. We would have to come to some decision, but we hadn't yet.

'Ought we to take the milk with us?' I asked.

Norris shook his head. 'I don't know. There's not much point if it would only incriminate Nancy.'

'And what shall we do with the gun and Harry's overcoat?' I found it something of a relief to be practical. As the morning brightened the nightmare was receding.

'I put the gun in a drawer,' Tim said. 'I held it in my handkerchief. I suppose it'll have Harry's prints on it, if we do need evidence. Was he wearing gloves?'

'No,' I said. 'It'll have Norris's on top, but we hadn't remembered that would be proof. I'll put his coat in the hall cupboard. If he wants it he can come and get it, but I have a feeling he won't be around at Victoria Lodge.'

'You may be right,' Norris agreed. 'Well, then . . .'

At that moment the front door bell rang and I went to answer it, leaning on the stick. My ankle wasn't as bad as I had expected, but it still hurt.

Under the rose trellis stood a policeman, and there was a police car drawn up on the gravel.

'Good morning, Miss,' he said. 'I'm Sergeant Wilcox from Henley. Are you Miss Timandra Warwick?'

I nodded, aware that Norris and Tim were close

behind me. 'Won't you come in?' I asked, scared and puzzled. The policeman was quite young and he did not look happy.

We led him into the living room, where the electric heater was still burning. We had not bothered with a real fire. All the coal and logs in the house had been used during the night.

'I'm afraid it's bad news,' Sergeant Wilcox said apologetically. 'We tried to get you on the telephone, but it seems it's out of order. Probably the heavy rain.'

'What's happened?' I asked sharply.

'Well, two lots of bad news, you might say. You – the Warwick family – have a chauffeur and handyman called Harry Cheam?'

'Yes.' Tim, Norris and I exchanged glances, but Sergeant Wilcox was staring uncomfortably at the window and didn't notice.

'And was he here with the family car yesterday evening?'

'Sure,' I said. 'He – he drove us out from London. My brother and me. Our friend came later and had some trouble finding the place. That was why he left his car in the lane.' I rather admired myself for my quick thinking. I didn't understand where his questions were leading, but he might have wondered about that.

'It was a bad night,' the policeman said slowly. 'Such heavy rain and bad visibility in places. Harry Cheam drove into a wall just the other side of Marlow. I'm afraid the car was a complete write-off and the driver was killed instantly. I'm sorry, Miss,' he added hastily, for I had given a small cry. It was relief, but he couldn't know it. With Harry gone part of our problem was settled. There was still Uncle Basil, of course.

'And you being a stranger and everything,' Sergeant

Wilcox went on. 'American, aren't you? Were you all thinking of returning to London?' He had evidently noticed the suitcases and Tim's painting gear in the hall.

'Yes,' Norris said quickly. 'We were going to spend the weekend painting and walking, but I guess the countryside is half-flooded. So we decided to go back to town.'

'It's not at its best,' the sergeant admitted, looking still more uncomfortable. He cleared his throat. 'Well, I'm afraid you'll find trouble at Victoria Lodge. The London police had a call from an old woman, Nancy Cheam, about nine-thirty yesterday evening. Seems she heard a shot and found Mr Basil Warwick sitting at his writing desk . . . dead. Shot through the head: a clear case of suicide. We understand there were business worries and the danger of immediate bankruptcy. A very sad case. Believe me, I hate bringing bad news. Are you all right, Miss?'

'Yes, I'm OK.' But I had sat down abruptly. So it had all ended with these sudden, violent deaths!

'And you, Sir? Mr Timothy Warwick, aren't you?'

'I'm fine,' said Tim, but he didn't look it. 'Thank you, Sergeant, for – for fulfilling an unpleasant duty. I guess we had to know. We'll get back to London right now. Our grandmother is hospitalised and not allowed to have visitors, but I guess we ought to get in touch with our aunt and our cousin George.'

'Oh, the London police have told Mrs Ann Warwick at her mother's house in Richmond, and I believe they have also got in touch with the son, George Warwick, who, I understand, is in Chester.' He said a few more sympathetic words, then departed.

'It's best this way,' Norris said, putting his arm around me. 'I kind of thought something like this might happen. Harry probably phoned your Uncle Basil from Marlow and told him the game was up, and so . . .'

'I guess we'll never know,' I said. 'Of course it *is* best. It's kind of a relief for *us*. But poor George and poor Aunt Ann! They'll have to face it all.'

'So you were right, Mandra,' Tim said, as Norris drove us toward London. 'It wasn't just your imagination. I'm sorry I didn't believe you. There were times when I almost did, but it seemed just fantastic. And then, when it came to the final danger, there was I . . .'

'Snoring,' I agreed, trying to speak lightly. 'Oh, it was awful!'

'Well, the worst is over,' Norris said. 'It's been bad, but you're both safe, and I guess what happened will be a secret now.'

'Yes, it must be,' I told him. 'No one else will ever know.'

I watched Norris's hands on the wheel, then glanced at his grave face. Without Norris we would both be dead and we hadn't even said thank you.

'You were the one who saved us,' I said. 'If you hadn't decided to come yesterday . . .'

'But I did,' Norris said, his eyes on the busy intersection ahead. 'Forget it.'

Norris and I . . . I sat trying to think of happier things, of a wonderful future, as we approached the outskirts of London.

I flew back to New York on 14th December and Norris was at Kennedy to meet me. I had told Uncle Serle and Aunt Esther all about him by letter, and they were simply delighted and quite happy to await me at home. In fact, it was a most joyful home-coming, only marred by the fact that Tim wasn't there with me.

I had wanted to leave London much sooner than that, but Mr Burrell had advised me to stay, as there were papers to sign and things to be settled. And I was really happy enough, sharing the flat in Chelsea with Tim.

Grandmother died quietly in her sleep, without knowing about Uncle Basil and Harry, and I guess it was best. So Victoria Lodge was empty, once Nancy had joined Aunt Ann at her mother's house. George took a room with a friend and started work at Warwicks two weeks after the affair at Victoria Cottage. By the time I left I knew he was doing quite well, and he hoped to marry his Ellie at the beginning of February.

Tim saw me off at London airport and the next day went to Paris, where he planned to study art under the best teachers. I knew it was inevitable that we should part, but it made me sad. Yet there were compensations.

Norris asked me to marry him as we drove back to Manhattan. It was frosty and growing dark, and we were stuck in a traffic jam. I said: 'Yes, please, Norris!' and we both laughed, but there really wasn't much chance of talking. He drove me to West 4th Street, but wouldn't go in then.

'We'll all meet later,' he said. 'You must come and see my parents and I hope soon to meet your uncle and aunt. But not now. They'll want you to themselves. Could you meet me at the office tomorrow at five-thirty and we'll have dinner somewhere and make plans?'

Norris worked in a building on Madison Avenue at the corner of 49th Street and we walked out into the rush hour crowds. It was a very cold evening, sparkling with frost, and there was an almost full moon. The shop-windows on Fifth Avenue were decorated for Christmas and when we strolled toward Rockefeller Plaza there was the great Christmas tree.

'Oh, I am so happy to be back!' I cried. 'Some day I mean to make another trip to London, but not for quite a long time.'

'We'll go together,' said Norris, smiling down at me. 'And I promise there won't be any nightmares next time.'

'George asked if I'd go back for their wedding,' I remarked. 'He really is doing quite well and they're both so happy. He's so grateful to me, but I don't think I'll go so very soon. George doesn't know, nor does Aunt Ann, but Tim and I mean to give them some of the Warwick money when we're twenty-one. Tim agrees that it's really our moral duty.'

Norris took my hand and we began to walk again. It was really too cold to stand for long.

'That's a fine idea. I have plenty of money, you know. I'm doing well, and a great-aunt left me quite a bit. When we're married . . . How soon do you think it can be? I know you're still pretty young.'

'Maybe in the early summer,' I said. 'I'd like to help Uncle Serle for a time. I did promise. Though I guess I could still work for him when we're married.'

'Sure you can, if you want to. Or you could get a job working with antiques, as you once told me you'd like to.'

I laughed and sighed. 'I would like that, one day. But right now I've had enough of Victoriana, at least. Victoria Lodge is going to be sold, Norris. Mr Burrell says there was provision in the will for that, and we only have to wait a while, until everything's settled.'

'It'll be torn down, I guess, and a smaller house built?' Norris suggested.

'Maybe not. Do you know that a Victorian society is interested in the house and most of the contents? They would like to turn it into a Victorian museum. And that's what Aunt Ann or someone said it ought to be, that first evening we arrived. Tim and I never went back, you know, Norris. Nancy packed up all our things and there was no need to see it. I'm sure I'll never want to again.'

'Do you feel the same way about the cottage?' Norris asked. 'I suppose you do, after what so nearly happened.'

'No,' I told him slowly. 'I liked that house, and the countryside. Mr Burrell is going to try and find a tenant for two or three years.'

'Then could you tell him for only a year? If you feel you could live there for a time. Nothing's settled yet, but seems my father may buy up a British printing works. If it goes through he may want me to live and work over there for a year or two. I'd be working near Maidenhead, and that's on the Thames. Victoria Cottage would be quite convenient if – if you felt you could live in the country and wouldn't be haunted by that awful evening.'

We had reached the restaurant on West 53rd Street, where we were to have dinner. I stopped and stood on the sidewalk, looking around at Manhattan. The lighted buildings rose into the clear winter sky.

I thought of the English countryside, golden in the October sunshine, of the beechwoods where Norris and I had never walked, the ancient villages and the wonderful manor-houses. The memory of those was, strangely, stronger than the happenings of that wet and misty evening. The Warwick nightmare was over and done with.

'I guess I would like to live there,' I said. 'Not for always, of course. We do belong to Manhattan, Norris. Oh, I'm so happy!'